ALSO BY DONNA COONER

Screenshot
Worthy
Can't Look Away
Skinny

FAKE

DONNA COONER

POINT

To Sarah Davies.
Your brilliance and faith changed my life.

Copyright © 2019 by Donna Cooner

All rights reserved. Published by Point, an imprint of Scholastic Inc., *Publishers since 1920*. SCHOLASTIC, POINT, and associated logos are trademarks and/or registered trademarks of Scholastic Inc.

The publisher does not have any control over and does not assume any responsibility for author or third-party websites or their content.

No part of this publication may be reproduced, stored in a retrieval system, or transmitted in any form or by any means, electronic, mechanical, photocopying, recording, or otherwise, without written permission of the publisher. For information regarding permission, write to Scholastic Inc., Attention: Permissions Department, 557 Broadway, New York, NY 10012.

This book is a work of fiction. Names, characters, places, and incidents are either the product of the author's imagination or are used fictitiously, and any resemblance to actual persons, living or dead, business establishments, events, or locales is entirely coincidental.

Library of Congress Cataloging-in-Publication Data

Names: Cooner, Donna D. (Donna Danell), author.
Title: Fake / Donna Cooner.
Description: First edition. | New York, NY : Point, an imprint of Scholastic Inc., 2019. | Summary: Maisie Fernandez has just about convinced herself that she does not care about her weight or her looks, or about only having one friend in Fort Collins High School (nerdy Owen Carpenter), but "Sienna", the internet profile she creates, is beautiful, skinny, and confident; the profile is part of her plan to humiliate the popular kids who bully and make fun of her, but suddenly the deception gets complicated—because the actual Sienna, the girl whose photos Maisie has been using, shows up in real life.
Identifiers: LCCN 2019007005 | ISBN 9781338239492
Subjects: LCSH: Obesity—Juvenile fiction. | Identity (Psychology)—Juvenile fiction. | Social media—Juvenile fiction. | Self-acceptance—Juvenile fiction. | Bullying—Juvenile fiction. | Secrecy—Juvenile fiction. | High schools—Juvenile fiction. | Fort Collins (Colo.)—Juvenile fiction. | CYAC: Obesity—Fiction. | Identity—Fiction. | Social media—Fiction. | Self-acceptance—Fiction. | Bullying—Fiction. | Secrets—Fiction. | High schools—Fiction. | Schools—Fiction. | Fort Collins (Colo.)—Fiction.
Classification: LCC PZ7.C78285 Fak 2019 | DDC 813.54 [Fic]—dc23 LC record available at https://lccn.loc.gov/2019007005

10 9 8 7 6 5 4 3 2 1   19 20 21 22 23

Printed in the U.S.A. 23

First edition, October 2019

Book design by Yaffa Jaskoll

CHAPTER ONE

If a fairy godmother, with raspberry-colored wings and giant chandelier earrings, suddenly materialized out of the beaker on the front table of Mr. Vance's chemistry class and granted me three wishes, I would not use any of them to be thinner.

That would shock most people.

I'm not skinny. Not even close. I don't weigh a few pounds more than every girl in this room. I am fifty or more pounds heavier than every girl in this room. It isn't easy being sixteen and fat. Even with all my monochromatic black clothes and minimalist makeup, it's not like I can hide my size. Just spend one day walking with me through the halls of my high school and listen to the moos and oinks behind my back. Maybe I don't think I'm ugly, but others do. I can't live in this world and not see how people respond to me.

My pencil scratches furiously across the paper. A plus-size fairy emerges out of the binding of my notebook. She has a phone in her hand to text me, because that's how this fairy godmother rolls. The bottom of her body curls like smoke around the silver faucets on the sink and then disappears into a row of test tubes. I change pencils, pick out a magenta one, and quickly color a tutu around her waist.

"Hey, Maisie." My best friend and lab partner, Owen Carpenter, sits down on the stool beside me. Owen is a tall, lanky boy with curly red hair and bright green eyes. Today, he wears an orange T-shirt that clashes with his hair. Owen is kind and thoughtful and more than a little . . . weird. In eighth grade, he ate Froot Loops for lunch. Not once. Not twice.

Every. Single. Day.

Middle school kids notice things like that and it doesn't go over that well.

I look up from my drawing. "Hey."

Owen leans over and says, "I heard Oxygen and Magnesium were going out."

Unfortunately, this kind of greeting is not unusual for Owen.

"And?" I ask, even though I don't really want to know the answer.

Owen grins. "O. Mg."

I stare at him. He did not just make that lame joke.

But he did. "Get it?" he asks.

The history of humor is Owen's latest preoccupation and he is currently obsessed with jokes. Really, really bad jokes. People might think it is his attempt at blending in, but I know Owen has no desire to "blend in." It's his superpower. The truth is, he is accumulating jokes like the butterflies pinned inside the glass case in the biology hall's insect collection. He told me yesterday, he now has 241. Thank God I haven't heard them all.

I roll my eyes and go back to my drawing. After a moment of contemplation, I add a green cat tattoo to the fairy's right shoulder. I box out a new frame, draw a close-up of the fairy's phone, and then print her text message out in block letters.

FAIRY: HOW ABOUT PRETTY?

Nope.

I'm concentrating so hard, I almost don't notice that the fashionably late parade has started. The popular crowd at Fort Collins High School prances into class, wearing their gorgeous skins and taking them for granted.

Dezirea Davis leads the pack, carrying her green Nalgene bottle. "OMG," she says to Leah Albertson, who's walking right beside her. "That new haircut is to die for!"

Leah looks dazzled by the compliment. She pats her new purple bob with satisfaction. "Thanks. You were *so* right about that new stylist downtown."

Dezirea beams. "And didn't I say that Kat Von D concealer was the best?" she asks acne-prone Casey Austin, who is trailing behind Leah.

Casey nods. "Absolutely. And it looks *amazing* on you."

Boom. Just like that, Dezirea gets the reinforcement she craves—an adoring audience.

Other than a brief eye lock, Dezirea brushes past my desk without acknowledging me. Not a surprise.

I watch as she takes her seat beside her bestie, Camila Ramos. In my high school, pretty and thin usually go together, but there are some exceptions. Camila Ramos is one of them. She's curvy, not fat curvy like me, but voluptuous curvy like Jessica Rabbit. She's stunning. And she knows it. Owen once told me that Camila is just lucky enough to have good genes and to have landed in the right society to find her particular blend of genetic soup labeled *beautiful*.

"Let's get started, people," Mr. Vance says from the front of the class. He's a big man with a pointy white beard and round glasses. He wears vests a lot and looks like a cartoon version of a snowman. He walks to his desk and calls roll, like he does every single day, even though he knows where everyone sits and could just check to see if there are any empty seats. Evidently being good at chemistry does not help you be more time efficient.

I tap my pencil tip against my desk, thinking about the drawing in front of me. I barely remember to raise my hand when Mr. Vance calls my name.

I hear Camila let out a cackling laugh at something Dezirea has said. "I can't *wait* for your party," Camila whispers.

Everyone knows that Dezirea is having a party at her house tonight. It's all anyone's been posting about on ChitChat for days. Everyone *also* knows only a select few will actually get to attend. Owen won't be among the included. Neither will I. Instead, I'll probably join the masses who follow along on our screens to see exactly what we're missing. Like the way I pick at my nail polish when it starts to chip, it's a horrible habit I can't shake. I peel off another sliver of Rover Red from my thumbnail, and return to my drawing.

FAIRY: THEN WHAT DO YOU WANT???

I look up to think about the question.

Jesse Santos glances in my direction. If popular had a poster boy it would be Jesse Santos, Fort Collins High School sweetheart. He has messy black hair, sleepy brown eyes, and tons of muscles finely honed by the football team's weight room. Jesse Santos is everything I hate about the in crowd—smug, entitled, and conceited. He walks the halls as if the crowds should magically part to let him through. The worst part is they actually do.

It makes me want to puke.

I look away first, dropping my eyes back down to the paper in front of me. I keep drawing.

FAIRY: WAIT. I KNOW. YOU WISH TO BE POPULAR!

I smirk. Sure, being popular, pretty, and skinny is the magic trifecta of high school. But evidently my fairy godmother doesn't know me at all. Or she isn't very bright. I draw a lightbulb over her head, but the bulb is dark.

Popular? Are you serious? Why would I ever want to be one of them?

Mr. Vance finally calls out Joretta Zajicek's name, waits for her response, and then stands up decisively and walks to the whiteboard, clearing his throat. The low chatter dies down.

"As you are all aware," Mr. Vance says, "Sarah Bodington transferred into a different chemistry class last Friday."

Sarah is a tiny blonde girl who wears a lot of purple eye shadow and sort of looks like a Pomeranian. Sometimes, she even wears a tiny pink bow in her hair, like she's just gone to the groomer. I think of her as a fringer. She's not quite *in* the popular group, but not completely *out* either. She was Jesse's lab partner in chemistry, and spent most of the time in class staring up at him with a constant needy look that reminded me of my sister's cat, Katy Purry, when her bowl is empty.

Like she had a chance.

Jesse always has some girl hanging on his arm, even though no one ever stays there long. As far as I know, Jesse's never had a steady girlfriend, although many have tried to score that hallowed spot. He's had dates, of course. Lots of them. Just look at his ChitChat page. It's enough to convince anyone he is irresistible. There are probably hundreds of girls in his pics—always smiling up at him with pure adoration. And he is always looking right at the camera with a halfway smirky grin I'm sure he practices in the mirror every morning.

Mr. Vance is droning on. "I realize it's an inconvenience so early in the semester," he's saying, "and this definitely isn't the best time for a lab partner switcheroo."

He laughs, but not surprisingly, no one else even cracks a smile.

Owen leans over and whispers to me, "Humor is often used to make light of a stressful situation."

"Except that wasn't funny," I whisper back. In the corner of my notebook page, I quickly sketch two beakers with faces, liquids bubbling out the top. One says to the other in a speech balloon, *"You're overreacting."* I poke Owen and point silently to the picture. He nods solemnly and I know it's going into his mental joke file.

I'm hilarious.

"But unfortunately," Mr. Vance continues, "because of Ms. Bodington's departure, poor Mr. Santos has been left all alone."

"Awwwww . . ." There is collective sympathy for Jesse's solitude.

Jesse swivels around on his lab stool to face the class and makes a big fake pouty face. He even wipes away some mock tears. Laughter from his many fans rewards him.

"San . . . tos. San . . . tos." Someone behind me is chanting. Like getting a new lab partner is some kind of Olympic medal.

I realize no one even seems to care that Sarah transferred to a different class. I'd be in the same boat. If I suddenly disappeared, no one would notice. Out of sight. Out of mind.

Some other voices join in the "San-tos" chant, but Mr. Vance finally shuts them down with a wave of his hands.

"That's enough," he says firmly. His eyes scan the room.

Dezirea raises her hand with a smug smile, volunteering. Beside her, Camila looks crushed, and even I am a bit shocked that Dezirea would abandon her best friend. *Is there trouble brewing in Popularity Paradise?*

A few other students put up tentative hands but, once they notice Dezirea is in the running, quickly lower them. When Dezirea's hand goes up in class, people pay attention. The fact that her participation is so rare makes it even more special.

Mr. Vance keeps scanning the room as though he doesn't even see Dezirea's hand. She frowns and moves it ever so slightly. Not exactly a wave, but definitely intended to get the attention she deserves in the coolest way possible.

"Maisie Fernandez?" Mr. Vance's eyebrows raise in question.

I freeze, pencil in hand. This isn't supposed to happen. I work too hard to stay out of the spotlight.

Dezirea whips her head around to stare at me, shocked he didn't call on her instead. Camila leans over and whispers something in Dezirea's ear.

"Ms. Fernandez?" Mr. Vance repeats.

"Yes?" I ask. *Please not me. Please not me.*

"Will you join Mr. Santos at his lab table?" Mr. Vance looks at me expectantly. Someone boos from the back of the room. Probably one of Dezirea's friends.

It's a question, right? Please let it be a question.

I shake my head and plant a hollow smile on my face as an apology. "I didn't volunteer."

Mr. Vance doesn't give up. "I realize that, Ms. Fernandez, but I think you'd be the perfect match for Mr. Santos."

An undercurrent of giggles immediately spreads across the room.

I'm mortified. The space around me seems to tighten and grow closer.

Mr. Vance nods at Owen. "Besides, Mr. Carpenter is quite capable of completing the lab assignments by himself. Unlike Mr. Santos."

Jesse mimes a knife stabbing him in the heart. More laughter.

Mr. Vance isn't asking me to move. He's telling me.

My throat constricts and something sour drops into the pit of my stomach. But there is no choice. I close my notebook and tuck it under my arm. Then I push the lab stool away from the table and the sound it makes on the linoleum floor mimics the screeching inside my brain.

My breath is ragged and quick like I've been running. Everyone watches, bodies freezing in place and all conversation stopping. I slide off the wooden stool. My face is perfectly still. Blank. I'm sure all of his friends will be commiserating with Jesse after class about this, but none of them will get the satisfaction of seeing me react.

I pick up my book bag, hoisting it to my shoulder. It feels like I'm throwing myself on the train tracks that run through the middle of Old Town. The train's horn is blowing louder and louder as it rumbles closer to my destruction.

The empty stool next to Jesse is under a window on the far left wall of the room, a million miles away. I pass a huge wall poster of the periodic table and almost knock a pile of books off the case under the windows with one hip.

"Timber," someone yells as the bookcase wobbles wildly.

Jesse stares straight ahead, no expression on his face, but I'm sure he's screaming in his head, *No. No. No.*

I haul myself up on the free stool and drop my backpack on the floor with a thud. I was perfectly happy in my own little world at the back of the room. Now the weight of everyone's eyes adds another unwanted ton to my body. I swallow hard, glancing over at Jesse. Remembering.

One day, back in middle school, Jesse passed by our table in the cafeteria, where Owen was eating cereal. Jesse had sneered.

"Hey, Froot Loop," he called.

Owen laughed. He didn't even get that Jesse was making fun of him. But I did. And in a flash, I stood up and Jesse was wearing that bowl of cereal. I remember exactly how that chiseled jaw looked when he wiped the milk off his face and glared at me. A crowd of awed bystanders gathered to eagerly watch what happened next.

"It was a joke," Jesse told me.

I stood facing him, my chin stuck out defiantly. Somehow, I felt lighter. At that moment, I wasn't afraid of

Jesse Santos or anyone else. There was a ripple of nervous laughter from the crowd, but I didn't back down.

"Oops," I said defiantly. "Sorry."

"Whoa," said a boy from somewhere near the back of the crowd, and I felt the stakes rise. I didn't say anything. I just waited.

Jesse blinked but didn't flinch. I held my breath, the blood pounding in my ears. Then, surprisingly, he just turned and stalked off, leaving behind sighs of disappointment from the bloodthirsty crowd.

I might have impressed a few people, but I couldn't stop the nickname train from rolling through the student body. Name-calling sticks and spreads in strange ways. Especially in the formative middle school years. So, after that day, Owen and I were forever linked. *The Froot Loops.* Sort of like a really uncool band name. Owen says it's like a superhero's origin story and owns it like a badge of honor.

Me? Not so much.

And that was just the beginning, too.

I shake my head, back in the present day. High school. Chemistry class. Staring down Jesse Santos. Again.

He nods at me. So smug. So sure of himself. "Hey, Froot Loop," he says.

Hey, Idiot.

Mr. Vance is busy setting out equipment. I see Jesse take out his phone and text something under his desk. I give a quick side-eye and catch a glimpse of a cow, pig, and elephant emoji on the screen. *Whoosh*. Sent.

Across the aisle, Dezirea raises a perfectly waxed eyebrow and looks down at her phone. Her fingers move rapidly to send a response. Jesse sneaks a peek at his phone, then laughs.

Seriously. Can't he be a little more imaginative? Pigs? Cows? Elephants? Don't you think fat girls have seen all that before?

I open my notebook. My winged creation waits impatiently for me to complete the story, her imaginary texts unanswered.

FAIRY: YOU GOT THREE WISHES, GIRL. PICK SOMETHING!

FAIRY: SKINNY?

FAIRY: PRETTY?

FAIRY: POPULAR?

FAIRY: WHAT DO YOU WANT? I'M NOT GOING TO HANG OUT HERE FOREVER.

I lean forward and fill in the waiting blank square. The truth is I would take all three fairy wishes and a million more—pack them tightly together into the palm of my hand like a fluffy snowball—and throw them all at just one thing.

I write the ending to my strip in block letters—the only thing in the final frame.

MAKE ME NOT CARE.

But I do.

CHAPTER TWO

At the end of the day, I wait for Owen in the front hallway by the trophy case full of tiny gold football players. We always leave school together and I give him a ride home. I put my backpack on the white tiled floor and lean back against the wall, watching the kids around me.

I know better than to dream, but sometimes the ideas just flash into my head. What if all the fashionable clothes fit me? And people genuinely smiled when they saw me, like my presence made them happier?

In this daydream, I'm not afraid to walk up to any group I see and join the conversation. The only thing I would worry about is if my hair *might* be messed up a little when my besties tag me in a photo. My back is straight, my shoulders strong, and I walk down the hall with a swagger of complete confidence. I like catching my reflection in the windows, and mirrors are my friend. Fort Collins High School is a miraculous world of acceptance where no one has to constantly apologize for their size.

Dreams like this are just a trap, I remind myself. *There is no miracle cure.*

Suddenly, I hate all the people around me, the ones that stand between me and my daydream. People like Jesse

Santos and his friends. They're not even here right now, but their presence is everywhere. I close my eyes for three quick beats, take a deep breath, and let go of wanting all the things I can never have. Then I open my eyes and do what I do best—use my artist's vision to refocus, and tamp down my feelings. It's the perfect wall between myself and the cravings that haunt me.

A splash of a girl's red skirt as she leans against a gray locker door catches my eye. Then I focus in on the pale face of another girl, chewing her bottom lip anxiously as she rushes off down the hall. And far down by the lockers, coming my direction with the afternoon sun haloing his bright red hair, Owen walks toward me. He lifts one hand in greeting and I nod in his direction.

"Let's go," I say, and we head to the parking lot.

☋   ☋   ☋

Owen takes forever to put on his seat belt—clicking the buckle in and out several times, adjusting the strap over his shoulder, and moving the seat up and back. I try to be patient, but I know the next phase of adjustments will begin after I pull out of the parking space. Air vents. Radio. Removing any specks of dust from the dashboard.

I sigh heavily, my shoulders slumping.

Surprisingly, Owen must have finally felt my mood, because he says, "You're unhappy."

"Duh."

"Because . . . ?" His voice trails off. He truly doesn't know.

I start the car. "Never mind."

"I'd tell you a chemistry joke, but I know I wouldn't get a reaction."

"Just stop." I shut him down, backing out of the parking space. "I can't even with the jokes right now."

I feel bad as soon as I say it. An uneasy silence descends on the car—a sure sign of Owen's hurt feelings. I should say I'm sorry. It might seem like he's impervious to my snippiness, but I've learned over the years that he's not. Instead, I concentrate on making it out of the student parking lot alive and without causing harm to another human being. A daily game.

As usual, there's a line of eager cars waiting to escape. A constant stream of kids squeeze between the bumpers and hoods, ignoring honks and yells. I pull in sideways behind a yellow Volkswagen, barely avoiding a curvy, auburn-haired girl carrying a huge poster that reads VOTE FOR SKYE FOR STUDENT COUNCIL.

"Hey." The girl holds her hand out in alarm over the top of my hood, almost dropping the poster. "Look out!"

"Watch where you're going," I mutter under my breath, but I let her go before inching up in the line. I glance over at the passenger seat. Owen isn't the cause of my bad mood. Besides, on most days, Owen is the only person I actually talk to in school, except when I have to answer questions in class. I can't lose that.

This joke thing will pass. Last month it was all things pi. At the end of the month, Owen was bummed that he could only recite pi to the 153rd decimal place. The record apparently belongs to the guy who could recite pi to the 67,890th decimal place. I should probably be happy Owen's telling jokes now instead of chanting out numbers.

"Sorry," I say quietly.

"It's okay." Owen has the tiniest of smiles on his face, his hair falling down over one eye, and he looks adorable. "You don't have to get it. Humor varies from person to person."

I wish I could say Owen and I became friends because I was nice to even the weirdest people in middle school, but that wouldn't necessarily be the case. There were two main reasons, and both were selfish on my part. My best friend since kindergarten, Louise Yang, had just transferred to a middle school across town, and the middle school elite had just discovered my second-best friend, Dezirea Davis.

Yes, *that* Dezirea.

I was left alone to fend for myself in the most cruel social setting in the known world—the school cafeteria. To make matters worse, I was on a diet where I ate all these assortments of weirdly portioned prepackaged foods that I faithfully took in my backpack every day for six months. This diet fell between the Protein Smoothie Diet and the Cabbage Soup Diet. There were always diets.

With this particular diet, I added boiling water to fake macaroni and it made a sort of pasty orange concoction. There was a tiny package of "potato chips" that contained four round circles of crunchy air and a miniscule spoonful of protein "chocolate pudding" that tasted like shredded cardboard. It seemed like a good idea to sit by someone who was eating something weirder than me. Owen never asked me about the faux chocolate pudding and I never asked him about the Froot Loops. It worked for us. It still does.

Now Owen busies himself with adjusting the vents and I concentrate on the traffic. When it's finally my turn to leave the lot, I pull out onto the road in front of the school and face the next wave of obstacles. We pass two benches overflowing with kids, book bags, various musical instruments, and sports equipment. It is like each of them have assigned seats, and the closer the bench is to the front doors of the school, the higher the rank. Nobody changes places. I can name every person sitting on, or huddled around, every bench and tomorrow they will all be there again. Once the weather gets colder, they'll move inside or congregate in a nearby coffee shop.

Before we make the right turn and leave the school grounds behind us, there is one final bench. It faces the mountains in the distance and away from the school, so it is an unappealing choice for all those wanting to see and be seen. Owen calls it the Thinking Bench. It has a bent leg on one side that makes it tilt so badly anyone could slide right off on those days the wind comes whipping down out of the mountains. If you look closely, there is a small drawing of tiny colored circles on the seat. Printed above the sketch, in black block letters, are the words *Froot Loops*. It's ours.

Evidently, no one told Grace Spencer the bench is reserved for Froot Loops or, more likely, she just doesn't care. Sitting there alone, backpack by her side, her feet swing restlessly above the ground like she's a child in a too-big chair. The air has a touch of the Colorado winter that is surely coming, but it isn't yet cold enough for even a thick sweater. Even so, I think her bare toes are probably a little chilly in those sandals. I wonder what Grace would do if we just passed her by and kept going. Would she eventually walk the two miles to our neighborhood?

"Are you going to pick her up?" Owen asks.

"Don't I always?" I mutter grouchily. I pull the car over to the curb and stop in front of the bench. Owen rolls down the window. Grace appears almost instantly, her smile warm and sweet as always.

"Would you like a ride?" Owen asks formally, just like he has done every day since Grace appeared on the bench.

Isn't it obvious? Back in September, I thought it was going to be a one-time thing because her mom's car was in the shop, but I was wrong.

Grace opens the door behind Owen and climbs in the back seat. "Thank you."

Grace always says thank you. She believes in gratitude and a whole bunch of other stuff that we don't talk about all that much. Okay, maybe I don't talk to her about it very much, but Grace talks about it a lot.

She talks about *everything* a lot.

Grace started at Fort Collins High School at the end of last year. Before that she went to a private Christian school, so I didn't know her. Most people are nervous on their first day in a new school, but Grace didn't seem the least bit intimidated. Not by me or Owen or Dezirea or anyone. She just walked right over to the Froot Loop table and sat down with me and Owen. With her messy blonde curls and perky smile, it was hard to ignore her. Then she pulled out a brown paper sack and offered us each an English cucumber and dill sandwich. They were cut in tiny diamond shapes without any crusts.

"I got the recipe from the internet based on high tea they served at the Queen of England's summer home," she said.

"Are you British?" I asked doubtfully. If she was, she certainly didn't have the right accent.

"No. I just like to cook and stuff."

I looked at the tiny sandwiches and Owen immediately took one.

Grace glanced over at Dezirea, sitting at the table by the windows. "Do you think she'd like one, too?"

I was so shocked at her nerve, I couldn't even get my answer out in time. Grace walked over to Dezirea and I watched, terrified. But Dezirea took the sandwich, bit into it eagerly, and then nodded along to Grace's animated explanation. I couldn't hear a word they said to each other, but pretty soon Grace came back and quietly slipped onto the bench beside Owen.

"What did she say?" I asked breathlessly.

"She liked it." Grace took a big bite of one tiny sandwich and chewed thoughtfully. "I think I'll try making scones next week."

And she did. They were blueberry. And she brought a little container full of clotted cream to go on top. After that, Grace sat with us every day, usually bringing a sample from some new recipe. She didn't seem to care that her social inclinations and sheer audacity could potentially score her a better table with a higher popularity ranking.

Now the car door barely shuts before she starts talking. Unlike Owen, Grace knows exactly why I'm upset.

"Being Jesse Santos's lab partner doesn't have to be a negative thing," she says. "It might be an opportunity to cleanse the bad feelings between you two."

Grace isn't even in our chemistry class, but somehow she knows this latest news. Grace knows *everything* about *everyone*. Lots and lots of random things. It's been that way ever since she started at our school. People tell her things about themselves. I don't know why. I think it's something about the way she tilts her head, furrows her brow, and just waits for people to talk. And they do. Like Camila once told her she's inexplicably anxious every time she's in a car that makes a left turn. And Leah told her she has a crush on Hunter Inwood even though Hunter is very clear that he's not into girls. And now here I am, talking to Grace about Jesse.

"Yeah," I say sarcastically, easing back out onto the road. "I'll just take a shower and wash off his superiority complex." Like it's that easy.

"I hear you." Grace plays with her messy ponytail. "But don't even pay any attention to that stupid meme that's going around."

I frown, stopping at a red light. "What meme?"

"Oh," she says awkwardly. "Forget it."

"No," I insist, reaching back for her phone, which she clutches in her hands. "Is it on ChitChat?"

Grace silently holds her phone out for me to see. The meme is on Jesse's ChitChat page; he's tagged in it, but I don't know who shared it. It doesn't matter. It's a Boomerang of me climbing onto the lab stool beside Jesse. Over and over again, I clumsily perch on the too-small seat of the stool, my body spilling out over the sides. If that wasn't bad enough, there's Jesse's reaction shot: looking directly into the camera. *So horrified. So repulsed.* The caption reads *"Jesse's new LIFE partner."* My throat constricts. Just by existing, by sitting, by walking—I am a target. I am reminded once again of how people view me. My body is a huge sign that reads KICK ME every day of my life.

Shame burns through me, but this time I'm not going down without a fight. My resolve to pay Jesse Santos back for everything he's ever done to me hardens in my chest.

"I'm sorry," Grace says. "Just so you know, I have faith in you. You're stronger than all of this."

Owen doesn't look at the video, but the smile is gone from his face.

I shrug, handing back Grace's phone. "I'm not going to be a *helpful* lab partner," I explain, driving ahead. "I can sabatoge him. If Jesse fails chemistry, then he's out of football. You know that, right? As his partner, I can take away the one thing that matters most to him."

"If you are his partner, you will fail chemistry, too." Owen doesn't even look up from the book he just pulled out of his backpack. As usual, he is all about logic.

"It'd be worth it," I mumble under my breath, but he's right. My lame attempt at retribution would only hurt myself.

"Keeping anger inside just hurts your heart." Grace moves her backpack to the other side of the car and slides up between the seats until her freckled, makeup-free face fills the rearview mirror. Her cheerful smile looks even more ridiculous close up. "Honestly, Maisie. Let it go."

How about I let you go at the next stop sign?

I don't want to hear Grace's thoughts on love and forgiveness. Especially when it comes to Jesse Santos. If she didn't practice what she preached so much, I'd pull the car over and kick her to the curb. But God knows, she's let *a lot* go with me. More times than I can count.

"You can't force someone to let go of something, as much as you think they should," I tell Grace. "You don't understand." The scowl on my face grows, but I keep my eyes on the road. "The meme isn't even the worst of it."

"So tell me," she says calmly.

To my surprise, I do. "On my first day of high school, the seniors in student council taped signs to all the freshman lockers welcoming new students to the school. It was supposed to be a positive Collins Culture thing. Natalie Vincent, the senior class president and super overachiever, even went so far as to personalize the messages with each freshman's name."

"That sounds nice," Grace says.

The memories rush back. "I can't lie," I say. "Those silly little notes gave me hope things would be different from middle school. More grown-up. More mature."

Owen nods, remembering with me. "My message said 'Welcome, Owen! Fort Collins High School is glad you're here.' And there was a tiny-sized candy bar stashed inside my locker."

A special treat for a new day. I still remember the look on his face when he saw me from three lockers down, wearing that proud little grin.

"My locker was on the top row," I say. "Taped on the front was my special message: 'Welcome, Maisie! Fort Collins High School is glad you're here.'"

I don't look at Grace in the mirror. Instead, I just keep talking. "I spun the lock, glanced around, and opened the door. And cereal poured onto my face like an avalanche."

I remember it so clearly. That avalanche of sugar-coated tiny Hula-Hoops.

Grace's gasp is audible from the back seat.

"It was everywhere, suffocating me," I go on, my throat tight. "In my hair. Down my shirt. Onto the floor. And under the feet of everyone running around trying to find their classes on the first day of school. It just kept coming and coming, until finally there was just a little pile of Froot Loops left inside my locker."

Just the facts. Don't tell her how you felt. Keep that part to yourself.

That day—my very first day of high school—it felt like the world was crashing down on my head in candy-coated slivers of hate and there was nothing I could ever do to dig out of the mess. I couldn't move. Couldn't breathe. Instead, I stood there in shock, trying to take it in. All conversation in the crowded hallway stopped and everyone stared at the girl covered in cereal. Gasps of surprise were quickly followed by laughter. I thought I was going to be sick.

My feet crunched the Froot Loops into a bigger mess with every step. My foot slipped and I stumbled.

Just get out.

My eyes darted around desperately for some escape and then focused on one laughing face in the crowd. Just one.

"Jesse Santos did it," I tell Grace now, remembering how his eyes met mine and how he stopped laughing, but the smile never left his face. *He enjoyed it*. "It was just a stupid prank to him. Some sort of act of revenge."

"For what happened in middle school," Owen fills in. "In the cafeteria." I nod. Grace knows *that* story.

"I realize being submerged by a locker full of Froot Loops isn't the worst thing that could happen to someone," I say. "Not by a long shot. But it . . . stayed with me."

It took forever to get the Froot Loops out of my locker, and out of my hair and clothes and books. And each little fragment of cereal was a reminder of why I hated Jesse Santos. And to this day, whenever I open my locker, I cringe a little, waiting.

"I'm sorry," Grace says quietly.

I stomp on the brakes to avoid a soccer ball and then again for a guy and girl who step out into the road holding hands. So enamored with each other, they don't even look in my direction. A gust of wind scatters leaves into a swirl of color across the gray concrete and I wait impatiently while the couple wanders slowly to the other side of the street. The trees at the edge of the road are just turning brilliant reds and yellows, stark against the foothills. Fall used to be my favorite time of the year—full of new beginnings and potential. Now it just means the cold is coming.

There is a brief silence in the car. Unable to stand it, Grace breaks it after only a few seconds.

"Okay, change of subject. Let's forget about all this

negative stuff. I have just the remedy. You won't believe what I heard today in homeroom." She stops and waits with a tiny smile for me to take the bait.

After a short pause and a right turn onto Timberline Drive, I do. "What?"

"Guess who *might* be coming to Fort Collins High School for homecoming?" Grace is obviously pleased with herself.

This year will be Fort Collins High School's fiftieth anniversary and there is a huge celebration planned for homecoming. Rumors have been flying about the identity of a surprise special guest—an alumnus of our school. I don't give Grace the satisfaction of a response, but my mind starts to buzz. Could it be the girl who became an astronaut? Or the gorgeous homecoming king from a few years ago who is now some kind of hotshot sports agent?

"Only your favorite person of all time!" Grace announces triumphantly. She definitely has my attention now.

"Lexi Singh?" I can barely whisper the name.

Grace nods enthusiastically. "Yep."

This even catches Owen's attention. "Seriously?"

Lexi Singh is not just my favorite person. She is my hero. She's the creator and illustrator of the popular Nosy Parker graphic novel series, which is like a mash-up of *Gossip Girl* meets *Wonder Woman* meets *Buffy the Vampire Slayer*. The series was adapted into a TV show, and it's what everyone is watching and posting about right now. All of

Lexi's characters—especially the girls—are independent and powerful.

I've copied Lexi's sketches line by line. I've watched her draw on YouTube and I've seen every interview she's given. I don't want to just meet Lexi Singh. I want to *be* Lexi Singh. The fact that she graduated from our high school only five years ago just makes her even more relatable. If she can make it, maybe I can, too.

Owen's voice startles me back to reality. "The light is green."

I drive forward. *How did Grace possibly know this before me?* I'm the number one Lexi Singh fan of all time. I follow her on Instagram, ChitChat, Twitter, and every other possible social media platform. I even Google her name randomly sometimes just to make sure I haven't missed anything important. There is nothing about Lexi Singh I don't know.

Except this.

And this is HUGE!

"You're serious?" I ask Grace, needing all kinds of confirmation. Kidding with me about this would be cruel and unusual torture.

Grace pats me on the shoulder. "Yep."

I push down on the accelerator, trying to keep my focus on driving. Grace gets on my nerves for sure, but if I wasn't behind the wheel right now, I would give her a hug. And I'm definitely not a hugger.

Grace keeps talking. "And I hear they are going to have a contest to select some students to meet her personally." She beams at me in the rearview mirror like she knows she's giving me the most amazing news ever. And what she says next hits me with a sucker punch right to the gut. "I think some kids might even get to have lunch with her or something like that. Can you imagine?"

Oh. My. God. Meet Lexi Singh? In real life? I. Cannot. Imagine.

Homecoming is three weeks away. My biggest dream could happen in three weeks. I might hyperventilate. I briefly considering pulling over to the curb and doing a wild happy dance on the sidewalk.

Grace seems pleased with my reaction to her news, but then the sound of "Amazing Grace" interrupts any further scoop she can share. It's Grace's text tone. *Figures.* She digs her phone out of her backpack and looks down at the screen.

"It's my mom. They're pouring the concrete for the driveway today. Can you drop me off at the building site?"

I sigh like it's a big inconvenience, even though I know it's only a block out of the way. Grace and her family are all working on a Habitat for Humanity house. They are always doing something like that.

"I'll give you a cookie for the extra trouble." She rummages around in her pink floral backpack and pulls out a baggie full of chocolate chip cookies. "They're my special recipe. I use milk *and* dark chocolate chips. Makes them super rich."

I shake my head. Now that my head is full of Lexi Singh dreams, I don't need cookies.

"These are way too good for her anyway." Owen smiles his wonky smile over the seat directly at Grace. He reaches for the bag and takes two. Grace looks delighted. He chews thoughtfully, then says, "If they were any richer, they'd be fortune cookies."

I do a serious eye roll and Grace groans. She twists a long curl around one finger, then throws it back over one shoulder.

"Too much?" he asks.

"You need to work on your delivery," Grace says graciously.

Owen laughs. "Maybe you can help me work on the timing?"

I look over at him in shock. *Is he flirting with her?*

Sometimes I draw Owen as a raven. His bright green eyes remind me of a bird. A lot of people don't know ravens are crazy smart and intense collectors of unusual things. Researchers even discovered that ravens use logic to solve problems. That's why a raven fits Owen perfectly. He is the most complex person I know. Brilliant. Funny. Irritating.

But maybe he is changing. If I drew him at this moment, he might shift into a rabbit—soft and adorable. The thought gives me an unsettled feeling in the pit of my stomach.

Once upon a time, Owen gave me my first kiss. It was at a Christmas party that my sister, Veronica, threw at our house. Veronica and her friends thought it would be hilarious to hang sprigs of mistletoe over every doorway, then shout at any two people standing under it to *"kiss, kiss, KISS!"* Owen and I were one of the first clueless couples caught unaware. I remember my heart racing as Owen leaned determinedly toward me. The kiss was more like two mouths awkwardly colliding rather than the swoon-inducing first kiss of the movies. Then we'd both pulled away, blushing, and together we walked over to the snack table to get more hot cocoa, like it hadn't happened.

"I think Owen likes you," Veronica said to me later. "He totally planned for you guys to stand under the mistletoe."

I'd rolled my eyes at that. I couldn't believe that a boy would like me, and besides, I didn't like Owen that way.

"He's not even a good kisser," I told Veronica, as if I was an expert, and she'd laughed and said that boys could get better at those things.

Now I wonder if Owen might have gotten better at kissing. It's been a few years, after all. I swallow hard.

"We're here," I say to Grace, abruptly pulling up to the curb beside a big dump truck. What I really mean is, *Get out.*

Grace insists on leaving Owen the remaining cookies. Then she takes forever to get out of the car, chatting endlessly about the cookies and the workers pouring the concrete and blah blah blah. I drum my fingers impatiently on the steering wheel.

Finally, she's gone. I breathe in deeply. Now it's just me and Owen again. We can finally discuss all the details of how I'm going to impress Lexi Singh with my drawings. But when I glance over at Owen, all excited to brainstorm a plan of action, his bright green eyes are intently focused on Grace's departure. And the look on his face sucks any joy right out of me.

CHAPTER THREE

I spend Friday evening alone in my bedroom, which isn't unusual. I love my room. It's my safe space. No matter how dark I feel on the inside, I always feel better here—surrounded by color and art. No blues allowed. Literally and figuratively. Instead, shades of yellows, greens, reds, and purples fill the room. Patterns of flowers, stripes, and checks adorn the bedspread and throw pillows in coordinating colors. When I escape here, it's all about hope and joy.

I painted the sunny yellow walls myself just last year and carefully selected everything, from the pop of bright red checked pillows on my bed to the green striped chair by the window. On my desk is a pile of Lexi Singh graphic novels and scribbled half drawings on various scraps of paper where I've tried, and failed, to copy her art. Colored pencils, markers, and ink pens scatter across the desk beside my laptop. My favorite Lexi Singh drawings of all time make up a collage on the back of my closet door. And my own completed strips are pinned on the wall above my desk.

High school might be terrible, but when my pencils touch paper, that all changes. On the page, I can create a reality that plays by my rules. And if I don't like the way something looks, I just erase it and draw it differently.

If only the real world worked that way.

But still. The news that Lexi Singh is coming to Fort Collins is almost as big as the Colorado night sky—endless with layers of possibilities. I sit on my bed, my feet swinging above my purple throw rug, my mind buzzing.

My sister's cat, Katy Purry, stares at me with a killer green-eyed glare from the open doorway. The cat blames me for my sister leaving her behind, but then, she never liked me much anyway.

When Veronica left for college in California, Katy Purry lay on V's bed all alone in her empty room for days until my mom finally started closing the door. The cat spent the next week sitting beside the closed door, shooting death rays from her narrowed eyes every time I passed to go to my room. Even the birds outside her favorite window could not draw the cat away from the obsession.

I get it. *I miss her, too, Katy Purry.*

Owen is rock climbing this weekend up in the foothills near Horsetooth Reservoir and out of cell range, so I won't even have his company. But maybe that's okay. While Owen supports my obsession with drawing stories, he doesn't really understand it. I'm willing to spend every single weekend alone, dedicating myself to the craft, if that's what it takes. If I'm really serious about becoming the next Lexi Singh, I have to make sacrifices.

Besides, I don't have anything else to do.

I get up and walk over to my desk, where I sit down and take out my sketch pad. My biggest creation so far is a collection of secret drawings that make up a comic strip I call *The Froot Loops*. I've never shown it to anyone—not even Owen. It's about my kind of people—the freaks, misfits, and outcasts of high school. It's a mash-up of oversharing and revenge therapy. Especially when characters shape-shift into wolves, dragons, and tigers and eat all the popular, mean kids. When I'm working on the *Froot Loops* strip, I'm not afraid anymore. And I'm not alone. This is the place I let everything go.

In *The Froot Loops*, Owen and Grace change into specific creatures—a raven and a dog. And I can change into anything. *Because, why not?* After all, it's my world and I can do what I want. It's the only place in my life where that is true.

The only problem? I can't draw myself before I change, only afterward—when I'm magical and triumphant.

In every story, I'm just a stick figure—a placeholder for my image that is yet to come. I can't seem to ever make that likeness materialize on paper. One strip shows a stick figure walking out of the lunch line with a tray of pizza. All the popular crowd sits in their usual spot over by the windows. They giggle and punch each other when she walks by. Then—SHAZAM. The stick figure shapeshifts into an elephant and sits on the end of the bench, throwing them all up into the air—expensive bags fly everywhere. A carton of yogurt ends up on top of queen-bee Dezirea's head, fat-free gooeyness splashing down her face. Tonight, I put the final touches on the girls' horrified expressions.

Then I go back to the stick figure and try to make it a real body. A girl who looks like me. Immediately the arms don't look right. There is an awkward bend to the elbow and the fingers look like claws. I scratch it out with big black marks. It's not even worth erasing. I turn the page so fast, it rips out into my hand.

I hate the way I look.

Instantly I feel guilty. Strong girls don't think things like that. They embrace their inner power and their size. I know because my mom tells me that all the time. Then my dad chimes in with his own words of wisdom. *Beauty is skin deep, but ugly is to the bone. Just shake it off. Don't listen to the haters. Be proud of who you are.* I read articles and posts and blogs and fashion magazines about body positivity all the time. I want to see it in myself, but I can't.

And if I can't see it, I can't draw it.

With a blank page in front of me now, I shift gears. I need something to impress Lexi Singh—matching her bold, confident style stroke for stroke. For inspiration, I look at a poster of Nosy Parker, Lexi's main character in the series, on the wall across from my bed. I glance down at my sketchbook, then back up at the wall, sketching quickly. It's not exactly copying because I give Nosy a completely new outfit—a white blouse, checked miniskirt, and black tights—and put her in a new street background.

When I finish, I'm finally happy. It looks like it could almost be a Lexi Singh original. Maybe I will somehow get a chance to meet Lexi, and then I can show her my drawings. And then . . . who knows?

I open my laptop, pull up a recent online interview of Lexi, and watch it for the fourth time. She's so confident and talented. Becoming the next Lexi Singh is not going to be easy, but someone at this very moment is creating the next big thing. *Why can't it be me?*

Lexi's life looks amazing online, but if I were to post about myself, it wouldn't exactly be prime watching material. But then everyone knows ChitChats are a reality unto themselves. Nobody tells the whole truth and nothing but the truth. My "truth" would look something like this:

draws picture *erases* *draws picture* *erases* *cries*
opens flap of blanket fort *crawls inside alone*

Nobody wants to watch that video.

The thought of ChitChat reminds me that Dezirea's party is happening tonight. They are probably dancing and laughing right now. Maybe they're even talking about poor Jesse, who got paired with the absolute worst lab partner. And Jesse is laughing and saying something like, "People like her are the reason I work out." And then they all laugh even louder.

But I don't have to imagine it. I can see it all for myself—in full-screen mode—and let the images build and simmer in my blood just like everyone else. Not that I want to be there. I don't. But I can only fight the urge to see what I'm missing for so long. I unplug my laptop and carry it with me to my bed. Once settled, pillows behind my back and head against the headboard, I open ChitChat.

Then I go to the party just like most of my classmates—as an uninvited and unwanted guest. It's easy. The Dezirea show is in full swing, broadcasting live on ChitChat with messages, pictures, and video clips.

At first, it's just morbid curiosity on my part. The Davises' basement is different from the way I remember it. Much more modern glitz, and much less My Little Pony. There is a lot of noise—laughing, singing, and talking. It's hard to filter out the sounds and where they are coming from, but from the continuous stream of A-listers in the background, it's clear that all the important people have arrived.

Dezirea herself appears. She's wearing a ruffled gold minidress paired with black sneakers and ankle socks. Her hair has tons of glitter and sparkle, with crystal diamanté bows pinned throughout her braids, amping up the glamor factor. Her brown eyes look even more striking with a thick addition of newly applied eyelash extensions. There is not a single blemish on her smooth dark skin. I watch as she puts on a glittering tiara that reads "Party Girl."

"I don't need to be waiting around like I'm some peasant," she declares to the camera. "I need to be walking around like royalty."

Giggling, Camila comes into the frame and tries to pull the tiara off Dezirea's head. Camila wears a simple sequined black crop top, a red moto jacket, and edgy white cat-eye sunglasses. If I wore an outfit like that, it would look like a Goodwill store threw up on me, but on her it looks chic and cool. Her hair spills over her shoulders in glossy, beachy waves. Outrageously pretty. I notice with a stab of bitterness the strip of toned stomach between the crop top and her jeans.

"Don't touch my tiara with your filthy hands!" Dezirea teases.

They both start laughing so hard Camila spits out her drink. Of course, that makes them laugh even harder. Then Hunter Inwood walks up behind them, wearing some outrageously green checked blazer over a blue T-shirt, and puts rabbit ears up behind their heads with two fingers.

Original.

A new video comes up. Another one of Dezirea's besties, Bella Carroll, snuggles up on the white couch next to a throw pillow with big red lips on the front. Everyone knows Bella is the richest girl in our school and tonight she definitely looks the part—wearing a Gucci ivory polka-dotted shirt paired with skinny jeans and nude stiletto pumps. Pearl-encrusted pins decorate her blonde

French twist like ornaments. She looks more like a twenty-five-year-old CEO than a sixteen-year-old cheerleader. She stares into the camera with a glitter-flecked gaze, and then Dezirea and Camila join her on the couch. Dezirea snaps a selfie of the three of them, and posts the photo to her account immediately.

DEZIREA: ALL MY BESTIES IN ONE PLACE! ALWAYS BETTER TOGETHER XO #BABESUNITE #GIRLGANG

Camila comments below it, and then Bella chimes in, too.

CAMILA: I KNOW I'M SO LUCKY TO BE THIS GORGEOUS!

BELLA: WHO YOU KIDDIN? I ONLY ROLL WITH PERFECTION

The ChitChats keep coming, the hashtags filling up my page. I watch them pour in and scroll up. #instaparty #musicislife #chitchatpic #lol #friyay

The stark difference between the unwashed and the it crowd plays out in living, breathing color. Because the only people who understand the funny references and in-jokes are there—*the chosen ones.*

I don't want to be there. What would I do? Stand in a corner and watch? It is no different than what I'm doing now. Not just at a party. Everywhere. In chemistry. In the lunchroom. I have to see exactly what I'm missing. Every single day.

A new ChitChat video from the party starts playing, and there he is: Jesse. He's standing with several of the football team members in front of the refrigerator, laughing about something. He wears a blue T-shirt that somehow brings out his brown eyes.

My stomach does a flip-flop. My shoulders tense, my mouth goes tight. "Oh, great," I mutter aloud to myself. "Just who I want to see."

Bella and Camila clatter into the kitchen, joining the football guys. One trips over the other, high heels tangled, and Jesse grabs Bella just in time to catch her before she falls. Instead, she ends up in a giggling heap on top of him.

"Oh my God, Bella. I can't breathe. Get off me." He pushes her off to the side. "You're huge."

Bella makes a close-up, horrified face at the camera. "Did he just call me *fat*?"

Then they all start laughing. It is the worst insult anyone can receive. Everyone knows that.

Bella is a size two and she's huge. What does that make me?

Ugly. Hated.

My spirit shatters. I want to strap a one-hundred-pound bag of flour to each of their backs and let them feel the weight of it on their feet, in their knees, on their bodies. I want them to feel it shift and morph over the sides of chairs when they squeeze into tiny desks and when they dance the night away under the disco ball in the basement. There will be no place on the planet where they will feel free and weightless. Not even in their beds at night.

Most of all, I want them to see how people look at them—if they look at all—with pity and disgust.

I shut down the computer. The black screen becomes a mirror. Instead of Bella's and Camila's gorgeous smiles, I only see my own fat, sad face. No matter what all the self-help mantras say, I am not enough.

I put the laptop on my nightstand, turn off the lights, and slide under my covers. I'm tired, but I can't go to sleep. Instead, I toss and turn, rearranging blankets and changing positions over and over. Finally, I end up on my back staring up at the ceiling, my hands clenched in fists by my side. I think about the meme of me sitting down on the stool next to Jesse. The ChitChats from the party replay in my mind like a movie projected onto my bed-room ceiling.

Why am I here in this world? There has to be a reason.

I want to believe I would step up to push the child away from the speeding car, to rescue the drowning puppy, to walk the old woman across the street. I *want* to believe it. But how can I be a hero when I don't even stand up for myself?

I understand cowards. They didn't start out that way. Something changed them. At some point something horri-ble met them as they stepped up to confront their demons.

Maybe it wasn't all at once. Sometimes the demons chip away at you, whispering and slithering their way into the strongest of hearts.

There is a tiny spark of something I don't want to face here with me in the dark.

It is anger.

And it is growing.

A tiny voice begins to whisper in some small part of my brain. It gets deeper and louder until I finally know exactly what to do. The thought takes hold and starts to grow.

Jesse Santos is only one member of the popular crowd. I can't take them all down, but he has a target on his back. Maybe I can't be the one to defeat him in my current form, but what if I shape-shifted into something else?

Or *someone* else?

I might be able to wipe that stupid grin off his face. Maybe I could actually make him care about something other than football practice and being cool and making fat girls like me miserable.

Minute electrical sparks tingle at my nerves. Adrenaline courses through my veins.

Wonder Woman doesn't fight evil as Diana.

Superman doesn't right wrongs as Clark Kent.

They change.

I sit up and turn on the light. My eyes wander over to where my comic strips hang on my wall. Dragons with glasses. Elephants with porcupine skins. Fairies with cell phones. Unbelievable creatures I can never become when all I really want to change into is a perfectly normal-looking teenage girl. A completely impossible dream.

Or is it?

I sit frozen, thinking. Katy Purry bumps her head against my hand. I rub the spot under her chin where I know she likes it most, and then I pull my computer off my nightstand. My mind races. The idea is still bubbling inside my brain. I think it over, scratching Katy Purry behind one ear. It is so wrong on so many levels and yet . . .

This is crazy.

Crazy awesome.

I turn my computer back on and open ChitChat. The best place for this little experiment to go down. I find the button for *Create New Profile*.

The empty screen with the blinking cursor makes me feel the same way I do when I look at the blank frame in my comic strip—powerful and invincible. There is going to be something here soon that has never existed before, and I am going to be the one to create it.

I quickly discover lying—I mean *creating*—online isn't complicated. It's like drawing a new character for one of my strips, but instead I use my keyboard. First, I need a name. Something cool and a little bit unusual. My eyes wander over to my desk. The soft reddish-brown color of one of my markers speaks to me. It makes sense that my creation should emerge from the colors I use for my drawings.

Sienna.

I write in the new profile name—Sienna Maras. Even her last name has special meaning to me. In some Scandinavian shape-shifting tales I read once, the Maras are restless children whose souls leave their bodies at night to haunt the living.

So appropriate.

Now Sienna needs a bio. Something catchy. I spend the next thirty minutes researching different websites and celebrity social media accounts. Finally, I write, *"Be yourself. Everyone else is taken."*

It's my own little inside joke. An Easter egg planted, but only for me.

I give Sienna's age—sixteen—and her location: Denver. Close, but not too close.

And now the most important part.

The picture.

I start to search on ChitChat for images of random girls, but looking for my perfect replacement makes me bitter. The more pretty girl pictures I see, the angrier I get. So many likes and comments. So much praise. They live in a world I will never know. I feel the anxiety rising in my throat, choking me.

Telling me to be okay with my body through perky Pinterest statements and Dove commercials doesn't change the way I feel inside. If I'm honest with myself, I would unzip my skin and step out of it. Just for a day. An hour. For a break. A breath.

Don't ever admit that to anyone.

For now, I give up on finding Sienna's perfect face. The picture is crucial, and I'll take my time finding just the right one, even if it takes me all weekend.

Then, still in Sienna's profile, I click over to Jesse's page and hit the *Send Direct Message* button. I take a deep breath. This is it.

For every oink.

For every giggle.

For every eye roll.

For every turned back.

For every stupid meme.

For every broken heart.

A shape-shifter steps out of the shadows and takes up the challenge.

CHITCHAT DIRECT MESSAGE

SIENNA: HEY YOU.

JESSE:

SIENNA: I THINK I SAW YOU ON CHITCHAT AT A PARTY. BLUE IS DEFINITELY YOUR COLOR!

JESSE:

CHAPTER FOUR

I roll onto my back and smile, remembering last night's creation. The birds sing outside my window. Sun streams through the blinds. Outside, I hear our next-door neighbor, Mrs. Deitz, mowing her lawn. Across the street, Mr. Alonzo's dog, Winnie, is barking at the fence.

My dreams were unremarkable. No werewolves changing by the light of a full moon or vampires flying away to coffins deep underground. But my resolve is still strong. I didn't follow nice people's advice about not letting the sun go down on anger. Instead, I let it burn deep into my sleep and trickle through my thoughts. And now everything is different.

Or will be. Soon.

Jesse didn't write back to Sienna's message last night, but I didn't expect him to, not without Sienna having a profile picture. I'm just getting started. My laptop waits patiently on my nightstand.

The smell of bacon distracts me. I sit up and swing my legs out of bed. First breakfast, and then I will get to work making the rest of my plan come to life.

Shape-shifters are cool in stories. The forms they take are awe-inspiring, powerful, and vicious. The form I will take will be just as powerful. In its own way. My creature's special power will be to make Jesse Santos feel vulnerable. And I'm willing to do whatever it takes to accomplish my mission.

Before I leave the room, I hear my phone buzz. I grab it to see texts from my sister. Usually, I text her on Friday nights or Saturday mornings, but I've been distracted. Veronica may be completely different than me, but we share a connection. She always worries when I'm just a little bit too quiet. And that evidently hasn't changed, even with the distance between us.

V: U THERE?

V: HELLO????

Taped above my desk is a picture of Veronica and me. I don't remember where the picture was taken, but we're both wearing bathing suits. I think I'm probably about ten, and she's twelve. She is laughing with a mouth full of braces and holds me in her lap, my chubby bare legs hanging over her knees. Our eyes are the same dark brown color, and our skin is the same light brown color. I'm sure anyone could see we are sisters. But while my face is round and pudgy, her chin is more pointed. Her cheeks sharper. She looks directly into the camera, eyes crinkled with her smile, but I'm looking up at her. It was so apparent in my expression: I thought she was amazing. Still do.

ME: SORRY. BEEN BUSY WITH SCHOOL.

V: HOW IS KATY PURRY?

ME: SHE HATES ME

V: AWWWW. POOR KITTY.

ME: WHAT ABOUT POOR ME????

V: YOU'RE FINE 😄

ME: RIGHT. GOT TO GO. DAD IS COOKING
BREAKFAST.

V: ☹ SO JEALOUS. EAT SOME BACON FOR ME.

ME: WILL DO

V: AND CALL ME SOMETIME??

I click off my phone and lay it facedown on the nightstand, then go downstairs and stick my head in the
kitchen.

My Filipino Californian dad is standing in front of the
stove and my white Texan mom is sitting at the table. My
sister's seat is empty and I don't want to think about that
too much.

My father's entire family lives in California. My only interaction with them is the occasional vacation and the big family reunion every five years that features an overwhelming number of *titas* and *titos*. My dad was ecstatic when a Filipino restaurant opened in Fort Collins a couple of years ago. It didn't make it, even though Dad tried his best to keep them in business. Now he just shops at the tiny Asian market located in a strip mall south of town and re-creates his family's recipes as best he can, but he always complains about having to buy frozen lumpia instead of fresh ones like his mom made.

"Good morning, Maisie," my mom says, glancing up from her computer. Everyone says we look exactly alike, but I don't see it. We both have the same thick brown hair, but Mom's eyes are blue while mine are brown, and her skin is much lighter than mine. My mom's family all lives near Houston and we don't see them any more often than the California side of the family. Whenever my mom misses Texas, she puts on George Strait music and tries to get my dad to dance with her. She calls it "two-stepping" and my dad just laughs and waves her away. She says she'd never live back there again. Too hot and too many mosquitoes.

"Hey, kid. Please put the plates on the table." My dad's greeting is quick and to the point. No kisses or hugs. On Saturdays, my dad cooks breakfast. Today, it's waffles. He leaves the sizzling bacon long enough to pour a cupful of batter onto a waiting waffle maker, then squeezes the lid down on top. Instantly, steam slides out of the sides and I smile at the delicious aromas.

Unfortunately for me, both my parents have short, round bodies that gave me a double dose of genetic punch. My dad fights his stomach with almost daily bouts of CrossFit. He looks young for his age, with a shaved head and a tribal tattoo that stretches around one large, beefy bicep. For as long as I can remember, my mom has embraced her size. Although she regularly walks a two-mile route every morning with a group of chatty neighbors, we all know she does it more for the social updates than the exercise. Mom also never lost her Texan true love of big hair and makeup even after living for years in nature-loving Colorado.

I open the cabinets and take down the plates. Dad automatically moves to the side so I can pull out the silverware drawer. My sister was lucky enough to inherit Dad's athletic passion. Her love is swimming and any sport with a ball. She may not be tall, but all that activity resulted in a strong, muscular body and the ability to eat anything she wants without gaining an ounce. V could wear every outfit I ever craved—prints, stripes, colors—but she will almost always opt for sweats and T-shirts. It's a constant frustration. Being big never stopped me from appreciating the art of fashion, it just keeps me from participating.

I think again about my waiting computer upstairs. I'm eager to get back to it and find the perfect profile picture for Sienna.

"You're going to have to put that away," I tell my mom, nodding to *her* computer. We both know Dad's rules about eating as a family and without distractions.

She holds up a finger. "Just one second. I'm almost done."

Mom is a professor in the education department at Colorado State University, and midterm exams just hit her inbox. She'll be in front of that computer grading for the next few days, oblivious to everything else. That means I won't have to worry about her being nosy about my plans.

I place plates, forks, and napkins on the table. I took out too many utensils. I'm used to being the younger sister, but now I am like an only child. *Am I still a little sister when the big sister is gone?* I don't know how this works. Evidently, neither do my parents, because my father has made way too much bacon and my mom has carefully left my sister's spot free of her work mess like there is an invisible bubble protecting the space. Being an only child sucks, but I didn't know that until it happened.

I take V's plate and put it on the shelf. The bacon is done and Dad carefully lifts each piece off the griddle with a fork. Then he hands me a plateful to take back on the return trip.

I sit down, putting the bacon in the middle of the table. Dad slides a waffle on my plate, then sets a jug of syrup down beside it. "Go ahead and eat this one while it's hot. I have one for your mother cooking."

Mom picks up a piece of bacon, chewing thoughtfully. Her eyes never leave the screen.

"I don't know what to do with this student," she says, shaking her head. "She's deathly afraid of gnomes."

"Gnomes?" I repeat. "Like, the little guys? With the white beards and red hats?"

She nods. "Yep. Garden gnomes."

"And that's a problem because?" Dad asks, coming back over with Mom's waffle.

I can think of a lot of reasons why that might be a problem.

"Apparently her thesis advisor is a collector of gnomes. Has them all over his room. Twenty-six total," Mom says. "She counted."

I try to think if any of my teachers would collect gnomes, but the only one who comes to mind is my history teacher, Mrs. White, who reminds me of Professor Umbridge from Harry Potter. Mrs. White collects cats. Cat posters. Cat mugs. Cat ears (that she wears every time we take a test). Cat screen saver. Cat T-shirts. I don't mind Mrs. White's cat obsession. It just made things awkward when we studied the idea of stereotypes in literature and Hunter Inwood said, "Like single women who are crazy cat ladies?"

What a jerk.

My dad puts the freshly cooked waffle on Mom's plate, then says firmly, "It is breakfast time. No computers."

Mom finally complies, moving the laptop and all her papers down to the floor. Dad slumps down into his chair with a loud sigh. I can tell he is in a bad mood, but then, everybody can tell when Dad is in a bad mood. And a good mood. My dad's pretty transparent with his emotions. What you see is what you get. I would have noticed sooner, but my thoughts are occupied. My mind is upstairs, already racing toward my new identity.

I put a couple of pieces of bacon on my plate and concentrate on carefully pouring the syrup on the waffle, trying to fill up each and every tiny little square to almost overflowing. I take a big bite and feel the warm sweetness explode in my mouth with every chew. Mmm. Katy Purry winds around my bare ankles and I push her gently away with one foot. She makes a small "me-owf" in irritated response, but it doesn't faze her and I give up, ignoring the furry tickle at my toes.

Unlike my father, I'm in a great mood. With the Lexi Singh news and my idea for getting back at Jesse Santos, the whole world has shifted. Such a big change since last night. Funny what a little hope and a big plan can do.

"It could delay the project for up to six months," my dad is saying to my mom, taking a sip from his coffee mug. Evidently the medical research project he's worked on for the last three years is not going well.

"You'll figure it out," Mom says.

I scarf down the rest of my breakfast, and as soon as I'm done eating, I say, "Can I be excused? I have a ton of homework."

My mom nods, obviously distracted by her conversation with my dad. Perfect. I put my plate in the dishwasher and head upstairs, Katy Purry trailing along behind. I hear the murmur of my parents' voices talking quietly from below until I close the bedroom door.

Time to get to work.

�   �   �

Believe it or not, you can research how to create a fake online profile . . . online. I sit on my bed with my laptop, and read through some good advice. Such as: Sienna's picture shouldn't come from a commercial site, like a clothing retailer, just in case someone goes searching for it. The picture also needs to be a little amateurish to look like the real deal.

So after doing some Google image searches, I realize that the models and actresses that come up aren't going to be good options. I go back on ChitChat and click deeper and deeper into friends' and families' posts—further and further away from all the people I actually know in real life. Nobody seems right yet. I want to feel something special when I see her face. A connection.

I don't want her to look *too* pretty, but pretty *enough* to attract Jesse Santos's attention. I'm not going to settle for the obvious. I know guys like girls who laugh a lot and wear perfectly applied eyeliner. Pouty pink lips are a must. But my creation is not going to be a knockout. Just cute and normal-looking. And she fits in everywhere. Sometimes she does really silly things, but she doesn't care what people think.

I'm already thinking of her as real.

I take a long breath through my nose and blow it out through my mouth. Then, suddenly, I see her.

The one.

Sienna.

Just like I imagined she'd look.

The photo is a full-body shot of a girl posted on the profile of a woman who I don't even know. The woman and I have one friend in common—my mom—but my mom never goes on ChitChat, so it barely counts.

The girl in the photo is not skinny, but she's not fat either. She has thick dark blonde hair that falls in loose curls around her shoulders. Full lips and magnetic smile. She poses with one hand on her hip and the other hand flung out toward the camera, fingers spread wide, as though she is telling the photographer to stop taking this gorgeous photo. But I can tell she's just kidding by the wide smile on her face. She knows she doesn't take a bad photo. There's no reason to really stop.

Her profile name says *"Claire,"* but that doesn't matter. I click through to her profile and find a few more photos— one of her wearing a pair of huge shades, her hair pulled up in a high ponytail, eating an ice-cream cone. Another where she's hugging a brown dog and they are both looking adorably at the camera. Then there is one where she is obviously dressed up to go out. Her eye shadow is dark, her eyes lined, and her lips perfectly red. She is wearing a short, boho minidress and over-the-knee, buttery brown boots I would never be able to pull over my calves.

My fingers hesitate on the keyboard. Then, before I can overthink it, I save all the photos to my computer for future use. Except the one where she's eating the ice-cream cone. That one I use for Sienna's new profile picture.

I am finally alive.

Suddenly I'm eight years old again, riding a bike down my street with no hands, laughing like crazy, and completely unaware of anyone watching or judging. I can be anyone. Do anything. I knew it. Shape-shifting feels like freedom. My shell of a body is loosening and opening all around me. I'm not trapped inside anymore. I'm in control of how people see me. Freedom tastes like the toasted marshmallows on top of a steaming cup of hot chocolate and it smells like the lilacs that bloom in my backyard every spring. It is welcoming and comforting and . . . attractive.

Sienna's picture goes up, but there's no response from Jesse yet. I do some more research, this time on how best to get someone's attention online. Apparently, if you want to slide into someone's DMs, it's all about making a connection. For example, if the person complains about a test in school, commiserate. Tell them you struggle with that subject, too. If they share a picture of a vacation, tell them you want to go there, too. If they share a new outfit, tell them how amazing it looks. If you notice them posting about a certain band, ask if they attended their recent show. And the advice goes deeper. When someone checks into a place, show up at a time when you're sure they've already left. Tell them they only missed you by a couple of minutes. Show an interest in the things they do.

Even if it's fake.

If I were really Sienna, I wouldn't think twice about sending messages to people I didn't know. I would be confident and completely sure they wanted to talk to me. Why wouldn't they? I stare at Katy Purry. She stares back, plainly thinking I'm the stupidest human on the planet.

"Jesse won't reply. There's no way," I tell Katy Purry. If cats could roll their eyes, she would.

My good mood and manic energy ebbs. This wild idea of mine isn't going to make a difference. Not in the big picture. People are classified as soon as possible and sorted according to a wide range of predetermined characteristics—looks, money, brains, friends. All the factors go into this socially acceptable machine and out spits your place in this world. It won't change. You can't change into anything different. Superheroes and shape-shifters don't exist in high school.

I turn away from my laptop. I could distract myself by *actually* doing some homework. There's a short story to read and analyze for English and a presentation to prepare for history. Instead, I pull out my sketchbook and work on one of my *Froot Loops* strips. Instantly, it's like magic pulsing through my fingers and onto the page.

In this sketch, stick-figure me walks into a crowded gym. It's a pep rally and the cheerleaders are dancing, pom-poms shaking, hips wagging while the crowd cheers. The chanting is rising over the bleachers—*"Go, team!"* in a bubble floating over their heads. I capture the elated look on each and every face.

Except mine, of course. Because I don't have a face. Or a body.

I can't get the sketch right. It's an oh-so-familiar problem—the one I have every time I try to draw myself into a story. I can draw me as a dragon or a wolf or a hawk, but I can't draw me as me.

I don't want to.

Stick-figure me squeezes into a spot on the bottom bleacher because I desperately don't want everyone watching me climb the stairs. The music is pulsing, and the cheerleaders are twirling and stepping in perfect synchronization. I draw Jesse Santos sitting on the bench with all the other football players. He watches the dancing cheerleaders in front of him, smiling.

I'm just finishing up the smug look on his face when my phone buzzes. I'm afraid to look. But then I see it's a ChitChat message. From Jesse. He replied.

My heart stops. I can hardly breathe. The fish has just taken the bait. Now it's up to me to reel him into shore.

Before I read the message, I finish my drawing. The rest of the strip flies out of my fingers onto the page. *SHAZAM.* I turn into a huge fire-breathing dragon, my scales the exact same dark blue color as the shiny pom-poms. I swoop down from the rafters and through a basketball hoop just for flair, then let loose a huge belch of fire that torches the GO, TEAM sign to ashes.

The last frame is the faces of the crowd, mouths open in awe. And one cheerleader says, *"Now that's a bonfire."*

CHITCHAT DIRECT MESSAGE

JESSE: HEY TO YOU TOO.

SIENNA: HEY.

JESSE: WHERE'D YOU SEE ME?

SIENNA: YOU WERE IN A FRIEND'S POST.

JESSE: WHAT'S YOUR FRIEND'S NAME?

SIENNA: IT WAS A FRIEND OF A FRIEND. YOU KNOW HOW
THAT HAPPENS. THEY TAG SOMEONE WHO TAGS
SOMEONE WHO TAGS SOMEONE ELSE.

JESSE: SO I'M IT?

SIENNA: HA. *TAG* YOU'RE DEFINITELY IT.

CHAPTER FIVE

On Monday morning, the fall colors are more vibrant than ever. The leaves on the trees are fierce jagged spots of red and yellow against the bright blue sky. The air tastes as crisp as an apple, biting and tart. As I get into my car, I feel as though I've woken up from a long coma. It's my world now and I no longer need to hide. Thanks to Sienna, I don't want to disappear.

Mr. Alonzo, our neighbor across the street, looks out his front picture window and waves to me. He's seen me coming and going since I was ten. He's retired and lives there by himself since his wife passed away last year. Sometimes, I even dog-sit his Great Pyrenees, Winnie, when he goes out of town to visit his sister in Florida.

"Morning, Mr. Alonzo!" I call cheerfully. He looks surprised. I don't usually say anything to him. I smile and drive away.

"You okay?" Owen asks when I pick him up in front of his house. He looks at me with curiosity as he gets in the car and adjusts his seat belt. "You seem different."

"I'm fine. How was your rock climbing trip?" I ask quickly, changing the subject.

"Awesome. I did the South Slabs at Greyrock." Owen loves climbing. The solitude and preciseness match him perfectly. The kinesiology and physics of each climb calm his busy mind. His lean frame moves fearlessly from hold to hold, the muscles in his back bunching under his skin, the only sign of the difficulty of his movements. I sometimes watch from below, but I've never set foot on the rock face.

"How was your weekend?" he asks.

"Good. Fine. Nothing special." I keep my eyes on the road. It feels uncomfortable keeping secrets from Owen. Especially a secret as big as Sienna.

When we get to school, Owen and I walk to our lockers. My thoughts are on Sienna and Jesse, and our last exchange. He sent me a smiley face yesterday but I haven't written back yet. I'll leave him wanting more.

I smile to myself. But even this small moment of happiness is tainted. I hear someone behind me say: "Wide load. Beep. Beep. Beep." As usual, there is no shortage of random people standing around, ready to pass judgment on me. Even when I mind my own business, saying absolutely nothing to anyone, some snarky person is going to comment just loud enough for me to hear it. Like I haven't heard all of it before.

Something new grabs hold of my body. A fierce, wild rage, like an untamed bucking horse galloping through my veins. Sienna wouldn't take this from anyone. I turn around and glare at the freshman boys standing beside the water fountain. One of them looks away, guilty. It is such a tiny victory. Almost not worth the effort, but I can't ignore it. Not anymore. I'm going to take up space, and not just on ChitChat.

Maybe Sienna should send a flirty message to that guilty boy, too. His acne-prone skin and frail build would make him an easy target. She would have him wrapped around her finger in no time.

Wait. I can't do that.

I know wrong from right, I remind myself. This isn't about lying to the whole world. *This is about Jesse Santos.* It's the only thing that justifies my dishonesty.

Owen and I are getting our books out of our lockers when Grace steps in beside us. She wears jeans, pink flip-flops, and a purple shirt that says PRAIRIE VIEW BIBLE CAMP in big letters across the front. She links her arm through Owen's, and that small movement is enough to set my teeth on edge. I want to tell her that Owen doesn't like being touched like that, but he doesn't look upset at all.

"Funny shirt." Grace gives him her most approving smile and Owen actually blushes. I glance over to see what all the fuss is about. Owen's wearing a T-shirt with a dinosaur drinking out of a cup. The caption reads *"Tea Rex."*

Seriously?

Grace links an arm through mine as well. I don't pull away. "I heard there is going to be a special assembly tomorrow to announce all the exciting homecoming details. Fingers crossed that Lexi Singh is part of the plan."

I feel a beat of excitement, momentarily forgetting all about Sienna.

"How do you find this stuff out before anyone else?" I ask Grace.

She shrugs. "It's a gift."

I shut my locker, and Owen, Grace, and I head down the hall together. Dezirea and Camila are hovering in the doorway to chemistry class. I see Dezirea flash a brilliant smile toward Graham Shannon, a tall baseball superstar with a killer fast pitch. He wasn't at the party on Friday, or at least, I didn't see him in the ChitChats. Now he swaggers by, flanked by two of his teammates. Dezirea giggles and blows a big kiss in his direction. He takes off running down the hall, hands outstretched like he's going to catch a fly ball. The crowd scatters, yelling protests but captivated by the action. Just before crashing into the lockers and a group of wide-eyed freshman girls, Graham claps his hands over the imaginary kiss and then smushes it onto his mouth in a grotesque imaginary lip-lock. The image is hard to shake.

"Wow," Grace says appreciatively. "He should join the drama team."

I sigh. There is no way Graham would be caught dead hanging out with the theater crowd. Evidently, there are some things Grace does not know.

The first bell rings. Grace says good-bye and heads to her history class down the hall. Owen and I walk into chemistry. I almost follow Owen to my old seat, but then I remember and stop short. Owen gives me a supportive smile and I smile back at him, grateful for our friendship. Then I turn and make myself walk toward my new seat. Jesse Santos is already in *his* seat, listening to something loud on his earbuds. My mood darkens instantly.

I slide onto the empty stool beside him, not making eye contact. I can feel myself start to sweat. *Oh, God.* Why do I have to be here?

But then something occurs to me. *Just forget he's Jesse Santos, überpopular football star, and look closely for the chinks in his armor.* I relax slightly. Maybe this is going to work out after all. As long as I'm sitting here next to him, I might as well gain some information for Sienna to use later.

So I watch Jesse, tilting my head and studying him like the elements in a lab assignment. He really isn't that good-looking. His nose is a little crooked and he has a scar over one dark eyebrow, probably the result of some old football injury. When he's not smiling, he looks more average. It's all attitude. Maybe this realization is something Sienna needs to know.

Jesse doesn't look my way, but I know he's aware of my furtive glances. I'm sure he thinks I can't stop looking at him because he's so hot. It's what he thinks about every girl. Even the fat ones like me. If only he really knew the truth—that I'm sizing him up for Sienna's purposes.

More kids stream into the classroom. Jesse's feet shift restlessly under the lab table, in time to the music coming from his earbuds. He clicks the tip of his pen—a relentless in and out and in and out. Finally, I can't take it anymore.

I lean over and yell in the direction of his closest ear, "Stop."

He pulls out an earbud and looks at me in confusion. The music is still playing faintly from the earbud in his hand—some kind of instrumental song. I motion to the pen in his hand and he puts it down on the table with a grin. That crooked grin makes me furious. He's the kind of guy who plays the slow smile card with every girl he meets. And greets every guy with a friendly punch to the arm and a head nod. And it works. People want to do his homework, or go out with him, or give him half their lunch.

Jesse pulls out the other earbud, then reaches for his phone to click off the music. The artist on his screen is someone named Trombone Shorty. I've never heard of him.

The silence spreads between Jesse and me like the puddle of dark stain on the ceiling tile above Mr. Vance's desk—slimy, ugly, and growing. If I looked down, I would see the oily spot creeping over the tops of my shoes. For a minute, I think about sketching and my fingers itch. It would be a welcome distraction. Last night, I started working on a new sketch of Owen, this time as a porcupine. The quills keep people away, but he is still adorably cute if you can just see it. Like I can. And now, apparently, Grace can, too. That thought makes me frown. I don't want to share Owen. Something so precious should be held close to the heart and protected. Like Thor's hammer or Wonder Woman's Lasso of Truth.

The tardy bell rings, and everyone settles into their seats. Mr. Vance takes attendance, then dims the lights and puts on a safety video about using Bunsen burners. The video features some cheesy song and stock photos of SpongeBob SquarePants and Britney Spears with lab goggles photoshopped onto their faces. Thinking the video will keep the class riveted, Mr. Vance uses the opportunity to go outside in the hall and talk with Mrs. Palley, the physics teacher, leaving the door cracked just a bit in case things get too far out of hand.

Immediately, Dezirea laughs loudly from two desks over, then looks over her shoulder at Jesse and me. She turns back to Camila, and they giggle some more, looking down at their phones. I try to convince myself they aren't talking about me. It doesn't work. I remember that stupid meme, and I clench my fists.

Distraction. I pull out a pencil and my notebook, drawing quickly across a crisp blank page. A round outline of a figure. Just a big blob. I know it's me, but I can't draw in any detail to actually make it human. Instead, I put all my energy into drawing an intricate zipper that covers the place where the face should be. In the next frame, I show a close-up of the zipper pulled partway down, revealing part of Sienna's face underneath—her hair dipping over one beautiful green eye. I have no problem drawing *her* broad forehead and thick eyebrows.

Jesse glances at my sketchbook. I quickly drape my arm over the top so he can't see my drawing. His eyes narrow with curiosity, but I don't give him the chance to ask anything about what he might have seen. *What if he recognized Sienna?* I snap the book closed and slide it into my backpack, staring blankly back at him. My world will never be an open book for his eyes. Jesse smiles and winks at me like he knows something about me. I don't break eye contact, my face motionless, and his smile wavers just a bit. Ha. He looks away.

You have no idea how good I am at hiding things, Jesse Santos.

Mr. Vance is still chuckling as he comes back in and turns on the lights, like the video is the coolest thing he's ever seen. It actually might be. He calls one person up from each table to get the lab materials. Jesse goes without even looking at me for confirmation. Dezirea goes up to the front from her table, and when they meet, she smiles at Jesse and hands him the material basket like he's just won an Academy Award.

When he's back, Jesse sets the box of equipment on the table and turns to face me.

"You're going to have to get over this . . . *thing* of yours about me," he says. "We have to work together, whether you like it or not." He rubs the corners of his eyes like he's trying to wake up.

"What *thing*?" I snap. Is he insinuating some kind of crush?

"I get it. You don't like me," he mumbles under his breath. He sits back down on his stool, crossing his arms over his chest. "But then, you don't like anybody." He turns his head to look at me, studying my eyes.

Has he seen more than I want him to? That thought is more unsettling than anything else. "I like plenty of people," I say, feeling uncomfortable from his scrutiny. "When they deserve it."

"Ouch," he says. He grimaces. "Nobody gets past that chip on your shoulder."

I bite back a groan. Who does Jesse Santos think he is? He doesn't know me. He doesn't know anything about me. Any doubt I might have about creating my lie online burns away like a dragon belching fire on an unsuspecting village. He deserves everything he gets.

He leans forward, filling up the space between us; I stare at him, not bothering to change my expression.

"Look," he says. "I have to make a passing grade to play in the game next week."

My cheeks flush with anger. "Glad to know I'm good for something."

"Not yet." He smiles like it's a joke.

I don't smile back. "Are we doing this or not?" I ask, slapping the lab assignment on the table in between us.

He squints down at the paper, frowning. "Do you understand what we're supposed to do?"

Does he need glasses?

He picks up the chemistry goggles, pulling them on carefully over his eyes and tightening the straps.

"Don't worry about your hair," I say in my most patient voice. "You don't need goggles for this part."

He quickly pulls the goggles back off, the tips of his ears turning red.

Is he embarrassed? Ha. I knew that would get to him. He's so conceited.

He frowns at me like I spend my spare time beating up small children for their lunch money. "Are you always so mean or just when I'm around?"

I feel a twinge of guilt and almost apologize. Almost. Then I remember the locker full of Froot Loops. The meme.

And, just like that, my resolve is back. I'm doing the right thing.

"Okay. What's the plan?" Jesse asks, and I can tell he's trying to remember something, *anything*, from our reading assignment.

The truth is, I didn't read the chapter either. I was too busy working on my history assignment and building up my Sienna profile over the weekend. "You're going to have to figure this out," I tell him coolly. "I don't do anyone else's homework."

"You could make an exception." He smiles and a dimple appears in his left cheek.

"I never make exceptions," I say firmly. This is like pulling teeth.

He rolls his eyes.

"Keep rolling your eyes," I tell him. "Maybe you'll find your brain."

He laughs. Not the reaction I expected. "Good luck with that," he says.

I just stare at him, sighing heavily.

"Look. We have to get this thing done." He points at the box of stuff on the table. "Can we call a truce?"

He holds out his hand and I look down at it for a minute in silence. I have to focus. There is no benefit to me keeping up this war of words when there is so much Sienna needs to know. So I nod and take his hand, shaking it firmly.

"Truce," I lie.

CHITCHAT DIRECT MESSAGE

SIENNA: HEY. HOW'S YOUR MONDAY?

JESSE: HEY! YOU'RE BACK. ☺

SIENNA: ☺

JESSE: IT'S OK. AM AT LUNCH NOW. HOW BOUT U?

SIENNA: I JUST BOOKED TICKETS TO SEE TROMBONE SHORTY IN DENVER NEXT SUMMER. SO EXCITED!!

JESSE: TROMBONE SHORTY???? R U SERIOUS? I LOVE HIM.

SIENNA: SAME.

JESSE: GUESS WE HAVE A LOT IN COMMON.

SIENNA: GUESS SO.

JESSE: ☺

SIENNA: GOT TO GO. MORE LATER.

JESSE: K. DON'T BE A STRANGER.

CHAPTER SIX

"Okay, people." My history teacher, Mrs. White, sits in the back of the room with the grading rubric and a red pen at the ready. She has on a psychedelic sweater with a white cat on the front. The cat is wearing red eyeglasses. I don't know why. "We owe our last group of presenters our full attention." She takes a sip from her Siamese-cat-shaped coffee mug.

I get the idea she's talking just as much about herself as her students. My stomach tightens with nerves. Now I wish I had volunteered to go in the first group of presentations, but I always delay being the focus of the whole class for as long as possible. It might not have been better, but at least it would be over by now. The presentations are about different countries around the world. Mrs. White encouraged us each to choose a country with some connection to our own background. She said it was to "personalize the content." We spent all last week on these presentations and I think we're all a little bored of hearing about Canada or Great Britain by now.

"Graham, you're up," Mrs. White says. Graham lets out a long breath, runs his hand through his hair, and stands. He turns to face the room, two spots of red flushing across his pale skin. He may be absolutely comfortable running through the hallway catching Dezirea's imaginary kisses, but public presentations are not his thing. It seems to trigger the stutter he mostly grew out of around the sixth grade. He starts out by showing his DNA report that proves he descended from Vikings. His country is Norway.

Grace, in the front row, nods encouragingly at Graham. Camila puts her head down on top of her folded arms, and Dezirea taps her feet under her desk, rehearsing some dance routine. At least Jesse isn't here; chemistry is the only class he and I have together this year. I smile at the memory of the Sienna messages I sent him during lunchtime, while I was in one corner of the cafeteria with Owen, and Jesse was sitting with his football friends at the other end of the room. Clueless.

Graham is still talking. I pull out a sketch in progress and get to work, trying to distract myself from being next. In the one frame, I've drawn Dezirea, Camila, and all their friends following a trail of bread crumbs to a Hansel and Gretel–like witch's house that's actually a computer covered in candy. Zombie-like—arms outstretched—phones in hands, they trudge down the path. Scrawled on the bread crumbs are messages:

"You're the coolest person I've ever met."

"I'm so lucky to have a friend like you."

"You're important."

"Follow me."

"I love you."

I zone out, letting Graham's voice fade away while I concentrate on my story. I pick up my ruler. When I can't think of anything new to draw, I make carefully measured-out frames across the blank page. Every empty square is a window for a tiny story that will eventually come, block by block by block.

It's the smell that brings me back to reality with a huge jolt. A strong, fishy smell that comes from a plastic container being passed down the row. My pencil stops moving across the page.

Camila puts a hand over her nose and quickly passes the plastic container on to Dezirea. "What *is* that?" she exclaims.

"As I said in my p-p-presentation," Graham says, annoyed that no one was paying attention until now. "It's l-l-lutefisk. Dried cod soaked in lye."

This is going to be a hard act to follow. I had hoped everyone would be dozing off by now and I could slide my presentation into the void without anyone even blinking. Now stupid old Graham has gone and woken everyone up with his fish.

"You have to at least try it. My grandmother sh-sh-shipped it all the way from Oslo," Graham pleads.

"Absolutely. No. Way." Dezirea hastily passes the container on. I sit on my hands, shaking my head vigorously, and make her skip me and hand it to Owen.

He takes a bite and chews slowly. "Interesting," he says.

Graham looks pleased. "And th-that's my presentation," he announces.

"Thank you, Graham," Mrs. White says. "Let's give him a round of applause, class."

People clap half-heartedly while Graham takes his seat. I rock back and forth in my chair, clenching my teeth.

"Maisie, you're up next," Mrs. White calls out.

To get an "Excellent = A" on the presentation rubric, I am supposed to present several facts about my country, along with slides. Mrs. White didn't say anything about bringing samples of food and handing them out like it's Saturday in Costco. I would have gladly brought in *balut*, a steamed, fertilized duck egg sold as street food in the Philippines. That would have one-upped Graham's fish for sure.

"Good luck," Owen whispers to me.

I take a deep breath and slide out of my desk. On the long walk to the front of the room, I don't think about my presentation. Instead, I think about how much I wish I was somewhere, anywhere, else in the world but here.

Too late now. I turn and face the class, clearing my throat. From this vantage point, the view is pretty depressing. Camila and Dezirea are looking at their phones under their desks. Bella and her latest crush, Leo Moore, are making googly eyes at each other. Owen and Grace are the only ones looking at me. For a minute, I can almost understand why Mrs. White turns to cats for comfort.

Straightening, I focus all my attention on the cat clock on the wall, counting out the seconds with twitches of its tail. Then I bravely launch my PowerPoint.

Just get through this.

"Here are some facts about the Philippines," I begin as I pull up the first slide, which shows a map of Asia. "Fact number one: For about three hundred years, the Philippines was the Spanish Empire's colony in Asia. That's why Filipino people often have Spanish surnames. Like, um, I do."

Owen nods at me, smiling. But even Grace is zoning out now, twisting her ring around on her finger. Everyone ignoring me should help me relax. *I don't want people noticing me, right?* Then why do I feel bothered by my classmates' indifference now?

I pull up the next slide: a painting I found online of a Spanish guy in a uniform and red sash. "In 1849, the Spanish governor, Narciso Clavería, sent out an order that all families were to be given a last name from a list of Spanish names in order to create a more organized system of keeping track of people." I switch to the next slide: a picture of the Philippine flag. "At the end of the Spanish-American War," I go on, "Spain gave up the Philippines to the United States. The Philippine islands were granted their independence by the U.S. in 1946, after World War II."

Oh, God. How lame is this presentation? I feel like I'm letting my whole Filipino side of the family down with these simple facts. I think about the things that actually matter to me. How my grandparents took me and my sister to the Philippines when I was five. I was entranced by the brightly colored jeepneys carting us through the bustling streets of Manila, and the tiny sari-sari store on the corner near Tita May's house. That's where my papa bought me my first halo-halo—a delicious shaved ice and condensed milk concoction. I think about how my grandparents were so proud of their first grandchildren and how everyone welcomed us so warmly into their homes. Family is everything to them—even a family that lives thousands of miles away in the United States.

I don't really want to share all that personal stuff with my classmates now. But I can still try to liven up this presentation. *What would Sienna do?* I wonder. I bet she would hold people's attention better than I can.

"Today, there are more than one hundred eighty languages and dialects spoken in the Philippines, but Filipino and English are the official languages," I say. "Tagalog is a dialect that forms the basis of Filipino." I look out at the zoned-out classroom again, and I remember the advice I got online when I was creating Sienna. *Make a connection.* That's what Sienna did. And I have an idea.

"*Magandang umaga* means *good morning* in Tagalog," I say. I pull up the next slide, which shows this phrase typed out in bold letters. "Why, um, why don't you turn to your neighbor and—and say good morning? Even though it's afternoon."

There is a pause, and I'm worried no one will do it. But then Owen turns to Grace and haltingly speaks the phrase. Grace giggles and says it back. Dezirea looks around to see everyone's reaction, but then gives it a try with Camila. Slowly, everyone else joins in, laughing at their accents and the feel of new sounds on their tongues.

They're actually doing it! I nod compulsively at each attempt. *They listened to me!* The feeling of power is like a jolt of caffeine.

My brain races. I need to keep the connections going, or I will lose them. "Of course, we all remember the excellent job Camila did in her presentation on Mexico and Li Na did on China, but did you know . . ." I flip to the next slide—a bar graph—and clear my throat. "Nearly four million Filipinos live in the United States, making them the fourth-largest immigrant group after Mexico, India, and China?"

Camila smiles, looking flattered, and Li Na nods up at me. The tightness in my stomach loosens. This isn't so bad at all. *I'm really doing this.*

I go to the next slide: a photo of a Catholic church. "Is anyone here Catholic?" I ask, and four students raise their hands, including Dezirea, who gives me a slight smile. "So you already have something in common with many Filipinos," I say. "Over eighty-six percent of the country is Catholic."

The final slide is a photograph of a bowl of chicken adobo, which is probably my favorite food. "The national dish of the Philippines is adobo," I explain. "A stew of cooked pork or chicken with soy sauce, vinegar, garlic, and peppercorns." I take a deep breath, then add, "Of course, if I were as thoughtful as Graham I would have brought some for all of you to taste." Graham looks up from playing *Candy Crush* on his phone to chuckle.

And that's the end. *I did it.*

"Are there any questions?" I ask. My legs feel wobbly, but I wait for the minimum number of seconds. No one ever asks anyone questions after the presentations. It's like an unspoken rule. But then I see Owen's hand go up and my heart sinks.

Not now, Owen.

"Can you tell me about the international tribunal ruling about the Scarborough Shoal reef off the coast of the Philippines?"

"Yes," I say abruptly. "China wanted it for the gas and oil revenue, but they didn't get it."

End of discussion.

It's over.

I pick up my laptop and head back to my seat. I see Mrs. White looking at me, clearly surprised in a good way. I am, too. I sort of . . . kind of . . . actually enjoyed speaking in front of the class for the first time ever. And I owe all of it to Sienna—my secret identity.

☞   ☞   ☞

The announcement comes just before the final dismissal bell. All the exciting homecoming events will be shared tomorrow morning in a special first-period assembly in the auditorium. So Grace was right.

"And best of all," Mrs. Buckton, the principal, says, pausing slightly for dramatic effect. "We will have a special guest joining us onstage. You're not going to want to miss this."

After school, the buzz in the hallway is immediate and intense. Possible celebrity names are everywhere. Whispered reverently. Yelled boisterously. Discussed intently. With every step, my anxiety increases.

Is Lexi Singh actually coming back to Fort Collins? Or is it that star football player who graduated a few years ago? Am I getting my hopes up for nothing?

ß   ß   ß

That night, I head upstairs right after dinner. I pull out my phone and do a search to see if there is any mention of Lexi Singh making a special appearance back in her hometown. *Nothing.*

There's a knock on my bedroom door and my mom sticks her head inside. She taught a late class tonight at the university and still has on her professor clothes—a silk blouse, black pants, and leopard-print flats.

"Hey, sweetie," she says. "Everything okay?"

"Everything's fine," I say.

"Your dad said you were awfully quiet at dinner tonight."

"Just thinking about some new ideas for my strip."

Mom steps inside the room and comes over to sit on the edge of my bed. The expression on her face is thoughtful and intense, maybe even a little sad. "You sure?" she asks, unconvinced.

My mom worries about me. But she also worries about climate change, gun control, women's rights, unrest in the Middle East, and our neighbor's dog who barks all the time.

"I'm sure," I say, taking a breath and putting my charcoal pencil down beside my sketchbook. For a minute, I want to spill my guts: about becoming Jesse Santos's lab partner and creating Sienna and dreaming about meeting Lexi Singh. It's all there in my mind, waiting to pour out of my mouth, but I don't even know where to start. Veronica would ask a million questions until I finally gave in and blabbed. But V is not here and I don't want Mom to worry about my lack of social life. Or about some dream of mine that is a big long shot and will probably end in a crushing disappointment. *Or* the fact that I've created this fake ChitChat account.

"Any drawings you want to share?" Mom asks, her smile warm and familiar.

I close the sketchbook, shutting her out. "Not yet."

She looks hurt but changes the subject. "I talked to Veronica today. She got into the math class she wanted."

"That's good," I say.

"She said to call her later."

Of course! I feel a rush of relief. I'll tell V everything. The thought of letting this pent-up balloon of feelings escape is so appealing.

Mom pats my leg and stands up. "Let me know when I can take a peek at your new creations."

I nod. I open up the sketchbook and pretend to be totally absorbed in its contents.

"Good night, sweetie." I hear the bedroom door click behind her.

As soon as Mom is gone, I call my sister.

"Hello?" she answers sleepily.

"Did I wake you?"

"I was just taking a nap." I hear her yawn. "Pulled an all-nighter last night studying for a philosophy exam."

"Oh, I should let you go, then . . ." My voice trails off. I shouldn't burden V with my problems. She has enough on her mind trying to make a success of her freshman year in college.

"No, I'm fine. What's wrong?"

I hesitate. Now is my chance. But how do I explain that I created a fake person online to get back at Jesse Santos?

And I realize: Veronica is thousands of miles and a new exciting life away from me. I can't tell her or anyone else about Sienna. Veronica would think Sienna was a horrible idea. My sister would never pretend to be someone she's not. She's all about physical, touchable, and real. Once she told me that my boundary between real and not-real has never been that defined. She says it's because I spend so much time making the images in my brain come to life on paper that I don't know the difference. Maybe she's right. But I do know I like the way I create people a lot better than the way they are.

There is no way to untangle Sienna from everything. Her short little life is now a part of me and I can't stand the thought of mixing all my feelings of missing Veronica into whatever it is I'm doing with Sienna.

"Nothing's wrong," I finally lie. "Just wondered how you're doing."

"Good. Busy," she mumbles. "Trying to keep my head above water with all this studying."

"Yeah, it sounds like you're exhausted. Go back to sleep, V."

"Thanks, M. I'll text you later. Love you."

"Love you," I say, then hang up before I can change my mind. I sit for a long time staring down at my phone like it's going to come to life with text messages and ChitChats from all my friends.

Surprise. It doesn't.

My finger hovers above the screen, and then I give in and log in to ChitChat. I did some quick research during lunch today and found out that Trombone Shorty is a jazz artist from New Orleans with a cult following. The touring schedule told me he'll be in Denver next summer, information I quickly put to use with Jesse. I learned some more stuff, too.

My heart flips over. I log in to Sienna's account, start a new message to Jesse.

CHITCHAT DIRECT MESSAGE

SIENNA: HEY YOU. WHAT'S UP?

JESSE: NOT MUCH. JUST STILL FEELING JEALOUS OF YOU.

SIENNA: WHY?

JESSE: YOU'RE GONNA SEE TROMBONE SHORTY! REMEMBER?

SIENNA: HA! YEP. DID YOU SEE HIM AT WASHINGTON'S LAST YEAR?

JESSE: NO ☹ BUT MY DREAM IS TO PLAY A HORN LIKE HIM SOMEDAY.

SIENNA: DO YOU PLAY TROMBONE?

JESSE: NO, JUST TRUMPET.

SIENNA: IN THE BAND?

JESSE: I WISH.

SIENNA: ???

JESSE: FOOTBALL PLAYERS CAN'T BE IN THE BAND.

SIENNA: WHY NOT?

JESSE: HAVE YOU EVER SEEN SOMEONE AT HALFTIME MARCHING WITH THE BAND IN A FOOTBALL UNIFORM? NOT GOING TO HAPPEN.

SIENNA: YOU COULD BE THE FIRST.

JESSE: MAYBE. PROBABLY NOT. TOO CHICKEN TO GO THERE WITH THE COACH. WHAT KIND OF MUSIC DO YOU LISTEN TO? FAVORITE SONG?

SIENNA: YOU'VE PROBABLY NEVER HEARD IT. I'M INTO SOME VINTAGE STUFF.

JESSE: TRY ME. I'M A BIG FAN OF THE OLD STUFF.

SIENNA: AT LAST BY ETTA JAMES—ONE OF MY FAVS.

JESSE: WOW. DID NOT EXPECT THAT.

SIENNA: ☺ I'M FULL OF SURPRISES.

CHAPTER SEVEN

I sit on the aisle, four rows back from the front of the auditorium. When I came in, I saw Jesse sitting in the back row with a group of his football buddies. I'm still processing what I learned last night—that Jesse Santos plays the trumpet, and sort of wants to be a band geek. It's shocking, really. I assumed all he cared about was football.

The stage is empty except for a huge screen and one wooden chair positioned off to one side. On the chair is a handheld microphone. I squirm nervously, swallowing so loud I can hear it above the chatter of the rapidly filling auditorium. Sarah Bodington, sitting in the third row, shoots me a look over her shoulder. I give her a smile and she turns back to the stage like she wouldn't be caught dead smiling at me.

Dezirea walks down the aisle with Graham. He wraps his arms around her waist and buries his face in her neck. She squeals as he begins to tickle her, oblivious to a whole auditorium full of people watching them. I wipe my sweaty hands on the tops of my jeans and press my lips together tight, trying to ignore them. Camila and Bella push past Dezirea and Graham impatiently and take their seats. Bella pulls a pink notebook from her huge wine-colored Marc

Jacobs bag and rummages around loudly for a pen, until finally Camila hands her one.

"I heard the special guest is going to be Wade Brown," Camila tells Bella. "He just got drafted to the Denver Broncos."

Bella shakes her head slightly, frowning. "I don't think so."

Grace and Owen appear and slide into the seats beside me. "Everybody ready for this?" Grace asks brightly.

Before I can respond, Principal Buckton enters from stage right and walks to the chair. She picks up the microphone, goes to center stage, and waits expectantly for the chatter to die down. She taps on the microphone. With each beat, I feel my heart pound back an excited response. *One. Two. Three.*

"Good morning, everyone. First, let's welcome our senior class president, Divinity Gates."

There is a smattering of applause as Divinity walks up and takes the microphone, flipping her thick black hair over one thin shoulder. Divinity is smart and poised—a formidable combination that demands respect from even this rowdy crowd. She gets right to the point.

"Hi, guys. As you know, homecoming is in two and a half weeks and it will be epic. Not only will we be playing our crosstown rivals, Rocky Mountain High School . . ." She pauses and the crowd obliges her by filling in the space with enthusiastic boos. "But it is also the fiftieth anniversary of our school!"

Cheers erupt on cue. Grace applauds enthusiastically and Owen and I smirk at each other. *Hooray*.

"Besides all the usual festivities—like the parade, the game, and the dance—we're adding something really special to our celebration." Divinity looks over at the principal and smiles broadly. "Now I'll turn it over to Principal Buckton to share the details and welcome our surprise guest."

Please be Lexi. Please be Lexi.

Principal Buckton nods and accepts the microphone back from Divinity. "As part of our homecoming weekend," our principal announces, "we're going to welcome back one of our most successful graduates. I know you are all excited to help me say hello to our guest today." She turns to look at the screen. "Lexi, are you there?"

I suck my breath in and hold it.

Suddenly there she is, my hero, her face projected larger than life onto the screen. Beaming in all the way from Los Angeles. Her features are so familiar to me—heart-shaped face, brown skin, thick black hair, brown energetic eyes. Her bright red lipstick and eyeglasses that almost match are super cool: definitely a look I'll try to imitate in the future. I would love to be able to see more of her shirt, which looks like it has tiny red dachshunds printed all over a dark blue background. Behind her are messy shelves full of books and awards.

She looks brilliant. Approachable. And completely, absolutely amazing.

Lexi holds up a hand and waves. "Hey, everybody."

"Told you!" Grace whispers, nudging me, and Owen gives me a thumbs-up. I'm too giddy to answer. There's an excited rumble from the gathered students. Everyone knows who Lexi Singh is. People might not be as obsessed with her as I am, but she's definitely famous enough to merit a big response.

"Welcome to Fort Collins High School." Principal Buckton's voice is enthusiastic.

Grinning, Lexi says, "Thanks. It's great to be back."

"So, what have you been up to these days?" Principal Buckton asks, settling back into the chair and holding the microphone close to her mouth.

"Nothing special." Lexi smiles and laughter spreads throughout the room. It's a huge understatement.

"You call having the hottest show on Netflix *nothing special*?" Principal Buckton asks incredulously.

Lexi shrugs modestly in a completely genuine way and another round of laughter ripples through the crowd.

"We are all so proud of your accomplishments and can't wait to have you back for our homecoming week," Principal Buckton continues. The audience breaks out in claps and cheers. "I know how busy you are these days and that you have some exciting news to share with us, so let's get right to it."

"Absolutely," Lexi says, sitting up straight. "My vision for Nosy Parker was formed by my life in Fort Collins. I realize people recognize a lot of the images and references.

It's not a coincidence that the town of Mountainview looks familiar. That's why coming home will be such a treat."

"And the rumor is you're going to give a few students the opportunity to meet you?" Principal Buckton asks.

Oh my God.

"No longer a rumor," Lexi says, smiling like she's revealing a wonderful secret. "I've had some amazing mentors over the years and I'd love to pay it forward and give some advice to young people today." She pauses for a beat and adds, "I will be attending the homecoming dance this year! And while I'm there, I will set aside time to meet with some of you."

An excited cheer goes up in the crowd. I clap as hard as I can, my heart pounding. It's really happening. Lexi is going to be here. And I could *meet* her.

"What type of things could someone talk to you about?" Principal Buckton asks.

Art. Drawing. Comics.

"Oh. I don't know. Pretty much anything," Lexi says. "Living in Hollywood. Working in the entertainment industry. Getting through high school. Whatever."

This time the excited cheers are even louder. I shift uncomfortably in my seat, the armrests digging into my hips. I realize the competition pool has just expanded to include practically every person in this room. Not just the comic geeks.

"So if someone was interested in meeting you while you're here and having some one-on-one mentoring, how would they do it?" Principal Buckton asks.

"I only have time to meet with a few students individually," Lexi replies, "so there will be an application process. Make a short live video explaining why you want to meet me. Simple. Then post your video on ChitChat with the hashtag #homecomingwithlexi." Lexi's rectangular crimson eyeglasses slip down her pert nose and she pushes them back up again, her brown eyes glowing. "I've already blocked out the time in my schedule and I will personally review all applications."

I suddenly feel like I'm choking. The thought of talking directly to Lexi on a video fills me with dread. I try to avoid pictures of myself unless they are carefully staged and filtered. I can't even look at myself in the mirror. A live video with no editing? *No. A million times no.*

"All videos should be posted between the hours of five p.m. and eight p.m. next Wednesday after school," Principal Buckton announces. "I have the permission slips right here, and they explain the rules." She holds up a sheaf of papers. "Just remember you have to have a parent or guardian signature in order to participate."

Bella pushes her glossy hair off her shoulder and scribbles furiously in her notebook. She leans over and whispers urgently in Dezirea's ear. I'm sure they're already planning their video masterpieces.

"So if you snooze, you lose." Principal Buckton laughs. *Seriously? She is such a geek and not in a good way.*

"Absolutely." Lexi nods. "And remember: Just look into the camera and introduce yourself. Tell me who you are and what you enjoy doing."

Principal Buckton faces the audience. "Easy peasy, right?"

Hardly. I feel completely overwhelmed. If only there were some way I could get Sienna in the video instead of me. But of course that's impossible. Sienna isn't real.

It has to be me, and somehow I have to get Lexi's attention. It's the only way I'm going to get a chance to meet her. I get one shot, and one shot only, to get it right.

⌕   ⌕   ⌕

After school, I wait for Owen on the Thinking Bench. Owen just decided to try out for the soccer team, which was a major surprise since Owen has never been into team sports before. He's super fast and soccer was one of his favorite self-study topics last year, so I didn't discourage him. But I can't help feeling antsy about how it will turn out.

I slide out my sketchpad and put some last-minute strokes on the final words of a strip I've been working on. I draw a big thought bubble in the next square. It's blank like my brain when it comes to ideas for the Lexi Singh video application. What am I supposed to say to Lexi to make her choose me?

I think about something I read once: that writing a graphic novel is about storytelling; it's just that 50 percent of the story comes from words and the other half comes from the art. *Maybe that's where I start?* My video clip needs both parts of the story—words and art. Both parts have to be perfect.

"Hey." Owen stands in front of me, flushed and smiling. Soccer must have gone well. He looks happy. "What are you doing?"

"Just drawing."

He settles onto the bench beside me. His hair is all damp and curly on the ends. He crosses his arms and settles back against the bench.

"How did it go?" I ask, glancing down at my notebook.

"I made the team." I can hear the pride in his voice. I look up from my notebook and see it shining in his eyes. "I guess all that practice I did this summer paid off."

"Congratulations," I say, smiling back, even though my stomach feels that now-familiar twinge at all these new things in Owen's life. *Am I really that possessive or . . . whatever? I don't even know what to call it.*

"What are you working on?" Owen asks.

For once, I don't hide the sheet of paper. I feel Owen's concentrated gaze, but I need to get used to people looking.

"Who is that?" He points to the blank face in the middle of the page.

"She's my main character."

"But who is she?"

If I say it out loud, then it will be real. But I need to. I'm the hero of my own stories. Right?

"It's me," I say quietly.

"Why don't you have a face?"

Every hero in a comic book has an origin story, and so does every villain. My origin story started in middle school. There were no secret societies, or magical insects that bit me and turned me into a special creature with extraordinary powers. Instead, I slowly morphed into what I am now with every pound gained and every mean comment. It was the perfect combination for a young girl's transformation in the shadows. When I hit thirty pounds overweight, the world made its mind up about me. I was fat. I would be fat. And that's all I would be. Category obtained. Match made. Face forever unimportant.

I shrug, then lift my eyes to meet his. "It's hard," I say. "I can draw *you*." I flip over a few pages and show Owen a picture of him as a shape-shifting porcupine.

He studies the drawing seriously, and slowly a smile builds across his face until he looks up to meet my eyes. "I like it."

"Me too," I say. "And I can draw Grace."

I flip over to a recent *Froot Loops* strip. In this one, Grace overhears two girls bullying a younger girl about her hairstyle in the school bathroom. I drew Grace changing into a yellow Labrador retriever with soft fur and a face that has to make you smile. When the older girls leave, laughing at their mean words, Grace noses open the bathroom stall. The last picture in the strip is the younger girl sitting on her book bag, her face buried deep in the fur of the comforting Lab.

I watch Owen's eyes as he tracks the story frame by frame. My heart thuds, waiting for his reaction. At the end, he laughs and it feels like someone just awarded me a prize. "Everybody in high school needs a shape-shifting Labrador retriever for a friend," Owen says.

I laugh, too. "Exactly."

"These are really amazing, Maisie," Owen adds, and all my anxiety about sharing my drawings with him slips away. "I always knew you were a great artist, but I had no idea you could do . . ." He gestures at the drawings in my lap. "*This.*"

His words make me feel like I matter. And now I want to tell Owen something I haven't told anyone out loud yet.

"I want to meet Lexi and show her my sketches," I say.

He nods like it all makes sense to him. "Epic."

"Thanks," I say.

Then he is full of questions because he is Owen. "What are you going to do in your video? What drawings are you going to show her if you meet her?"

I shut my eyes and shake my head. "I don't know what I'm going to do yet, and it's making me crazy."

"Can I help?" he asks.

I shrug. "I don't think so, but I'll keep you posted."

He pats me awkwardly on the shoulder. "You'll figure it all out."

But what if I don't?

⌕   ⌕   ⌕

That night, my parents go to bed early. I walk around the house, but I can't settle. I turn on the television and turn it off again. I open the fridge and stare inside. Finally, I take out a container of strawberry yogurt and bring it up to my room.

I sit down on my bed with my sketches. Katy Purry rubs her head against my hand, demanding I scratch her under her chin just where she likes it. When I don't respond, she looks up at me with intense green eyes and waits, staring. Finally, I give in and pat her head. My touch isn't right. Evidently, I don't do it like Veronica. But then, I don't do anything like Veronica. The cat gives me an impatient glare, then rolls over on her back.

"I'm busy," I tell her.

Cats don't understand busy. She twists and turns, paws waving in the air, shedding black fur across my bedspread. I reach out and rub her soft, furry stomach. Definitely not what she wanted. My kindness is rewarded with a swipe of one white paw.

"Ouch!" I yell, shaking my hand. It now features two angry scratches across the back. Katy Purry jumps off the bed and stalks across the room, to lick wildly at her fur as though my brief tummy pat was incredibly rude. My relationship with Katy Purry continues to be rocky.

I give up on building cat relations and spread some of my sketches across my bed like tiles on a floor. What did

Lexi say? *Look into the camera and introduce yourself. Tell me who you are and what you enjoy doing.*

What do I say? I stare down at the images of dragons, werewolves, monsters, dogs, porcupines, ravens, and masked superheroes, but there is no *me* anywhere in any of these pictures. How does an invisible person create a video of themselves? I sweep the papers off the bed in frustration, then reach for my computer.

I log on to Sienna's account, staring at her profile picture for a long time. *This* is a mask I can hide behind. Is this how Clark Kent feels just before he runs into the phone booth to change into Superman?

There is still one problem with Sienna. My eyes lock onto the little number 0 icon in the right-hand corner of her profile. No popular ChitChat girl is going to have absolutely no friends. She may look perfect, but I need more to make Jesse believe she's a real person. I have to fix that and fast, but Sienna's friends also need to be as special as she is. I need the *right* people. And I have to find photos of these right people—people I don't know—and post them to ChitChat, give them fake names, and connect them all to each other with an elaborate series of messages about their various activities together. *Simple, right?*

I spend the next hour creating two friends for Sienna— her besties. I name the first one Brittany, because it's a pretty common name. I know of at least three Brittanys in our school. Finding "Brittany's" picture is a little harder. Finally, I settle on a girl I see in a pop-up ad for a miracle face wash that promises to be an "oily skin game changer." I use the "before" picture with a few blemishes for Brittany's profile pic, thinking she looks more realistic that way as a regular high school girl. It's important for her to look good— just not as good as Sienna. Sort of a Robin to Sienna's Batman.

Brittany is on the swim team and her profile quote says, *"Just keep swimming."* She also loves K-pop bands and cat videos. The pictures and videos she posts are mostly of her brightly painted toenails in front of beaches and swimming pools. I decide it's her thing because I don't have any more pictures of her face. Sienna leaves a comment under Brittany's picture:

I CAN'T BELIEVE YOU'RE GOING TO BARBADOS FOR THANKSGIVING! I'M SO SO SO JEALOUS!

It makes me nervous to see how few pictures I have on Brittany's profile. One picture of a face model is not realistic. So for the second bestie—I name her Kira—I return to the profile of the "real" Sienna: Claire. I pick one of her actual friends: a skinny, dark-eyed girl. This way, I can post photos of the two of them together, and it's much easier to create a more believable friendship. In my world, Kira is a huge fan of fantasy novels, loves pop culture, and is active in student government. Sienna posts a comment on Kira's page:

LET'S SEE THE NEW AVENGERS MOVIE ON FRIDAY? GIRLS' NIGHT???

But I have to go further. Connecting Sienna with people Jesse actually knows is the best way to make him believe she is real. So now Sienna just needs to friend some friends of Jesse. Luckily, I know just the right person to help me connect my web.

Once upon a time, Dezirea and I were good friends. We were inseparable in elementary school. Sleepovers. Birthday parties. Bike rides to each other's houses. Secrets shared.

In fifth grade, our class went up to the mountains for Eco Week. It was supposed to teach us about nature and teamwork. Owen discovered his passion and natural ability for rock climbing. I learned something different.

All week, we played team-building games. The culminating activity was a long hike straight up to the top of a mountain. The instructors added rules: Everyone had a team. If one member of the team needed a break, then another member of the team had to stop and wait with them. No one would be left on the mountainside alone.

I'm sure that seemed like a good idea to the camp leaders. Everyone would rally around and support each person on the team to achieve the goal of getting to the top. But the reality was, it just put a target on my back. No one wanted me on their team because everyone knew I wasn't going to make it to the summit. Being my friend meant instant disappointment and ultimate failure.

It was bad enough having to balance on ropes and trust-fall into people's arms who were supposed to catch you, but this hike kept me up all night worrying. In the girls' cabin, I'd stare at the springs on the top bunk and listen to Penelope Young snore above me. The night before the hike, I slid out of bed, put on my slippers, and snuck outside into the darkness. I looked up to see a billion stars— layers upon layers upon layers. My breath clouded into puffs while I sat on a fallen log, shivering in my pajamas. In that moment, it was like something tiny inside me became bigger and more beautiful than anything I'd ever imagined. All the tension from the day poured out into the starry, cold night. This was the mountain experience I needed. *Breathing in. Breathing out.*

Suddenly, Dezirea was there, in black fleece leggings and sheepskin Minnetonka slides, a red plaid blanket wrapped around her shoulders. She sank down beside me and draped the warmth of the blanket over my shivering shoulders.

"I won't leave you behind tomorrow," she said quietly.

I frowned. "But then you won't get to the top."

She laughed. "Like I care?"

I slipped my arm through hers and laid my head on her shoulder. "What did I do to deserve you?"

She shrugged, but even in the dark, I could see the tiny quirk of her lips.

We sat there huddled together on that log for a long, quiet moment.

Finally, Dezirea said, "All this fresh air makes me hungry."

I laughed. "Okay, now you just ruined the moment."

But actually that comment was perfectly Dezirea, and that made it just right.

I look at her ChitChat profile picture now, and can't find the familiar face beneath her shiny, polished features. She's changed. We both have. The years between then and now snapped the bold edges off my life and layered them onto hers. I don't hate the *me* inside my body. Far from it. I know that I'm smart, occasionally funny, and talented. It's just the disguise I live inside that I hate. That's not Dezirea's fault.

When we were younger, Dezirea's biggest dream was to become a ballet dancer. She had posters above her bed of Misty Copeland and Lauren Anderson—Black ballerinas who took the dancing world by storm and broke barriers for other young dancers. Dezirea idolized everything about them. I remember sitting on her bed and watching her leap gracefully around her bedroom, only she called it doing a grand jeté. I called it amazing.

I search through Dezirea's photos, pictures, and posts. Finally, I take a chance and go for it.

SIENNA: LOVE LOVE LOVE THE MISTY COPELAND LACE
CROP YOU'RE WEARING IN THIS PHOTO!!! SERIOUSLY,
YOU SHOULD MODEL FOR HER NEW UNDER ARMOUR LINE.

I wait. The suspense is killing me.

DEZIREA: SHE IS MY HERO.

Ah. There she is. My breath whooshes out in relief and a smile tugs at my lips.

SIENNA: I CAN UNDERSTAND WHY. SHE'S AMAZING. YOU KIND OF LOOK LIKE HER.

DEZIREA: YOU THINK SO?

SIENNA: TOTALLY.

There is a pause and Dezirea must be doing her own research into this new Sienna person. I feel a well of panic rise up suddenly in my chest. Two followers is not enough. *What if she doesn't write back? Ever?*

I move on to Camila's profile. She's just posted a Boomerang video where she smooches the screen over and over again. I write a comment under it.

SIENNA: DYING TO KNOW THE SHADE OF LIPSTICK YOU'RE WEARING! IT'S PERFECT.

No response yet. I go over to Bella's profile. She's just posted about a recent trip with her parents to New York City. She stands giving a thumbs-up underneath the marquee of the *Mean Girls* Broadway show.

Her caption reads: WANT TO JOIN ME? OOPS. SO
SORRY. SOLD OUT.

Typically smug. I type out a quick comment.

SIENNA: SO GOOD! DID YOU GET TO SEE THE ORIGINAL
CAST?

I click over to Graham's profile. I wade through some
videos of sports practice until I see a photo of him at a concert at the Aggie Theatre.

SIENNA: I WAS AT THIS SHOW, TOO! DID YOU GET CLOSE
TO THE STAGE?

Hunter Inwood is a little harder to crack. I scroll
through his videos, pictures, and posts, but nothing strikes
a chord. Finally, I settle on a pretty generic comment and
hope it gets enough attention for a follow.

SIENNA: YOUR MEME GAME IS THE BEST!

Then I write a new post on Sienna's own profile, just to
see if anyone out there is watching.

SIENNA: HEY FORT COLLINS PEEPS! I'M IN TOWN. HIT ME UP.

Almost immediately, I get a reply.

DEZIREA: CAN'T BELIEVE YOU'RE HERE! COME MEET US AT THE MALL!

What would Sienna say? My mind races. *Be cool.*

SIENNA: OH MAN! I WAS JUST THERE. WE JUST MISSED EACH OTHER! NEXT TIME?

I can't do anything more or I'll just look like some internet stalker. All I can do now is wait. I pick up the yogurt off my nightstand and stir it slowly, blending in all the strawberries from the bottom until it's the perfect color of pale pink. Smiling, I take a bite, letting the tangy sweetness melt into my mouth.

Fortunately, I don't have to wait long for someone else to chat with Sienna. A new message pops up in my inbox. It's from Jesse.

CHITCHAT DIRECT MESSAGE

JESSE: THINKING OF YOU.

SIENNA: NICE. WHY?

JESSE: I'M LISTENING TO SOME TROMBONE SHORTY RN.

SIENNA: WHY DO YOU LIKE JAZZ?

JESSE: DON'T LIKE. LOOOOOOOOOOVE IT.

SIENNA: BUT WHY?

JESSE: BIG QUESTION. HARD TO ANSWER. I GUESS CAUSE IT'S MOSTLY IMPROVISED, YOU KNOW? SO YOU CREATE ART EVERY TIME YOU PLAY. DOES THAT MAKE SENSE?

SIENNA: TOTALLY. CREATIVITY IS EVERYTHING.

JESSE: YEAH. PLUS, IN JAZZ REAL PEOPLE PLAY REAL INSTRUMENTS. NOT COMPUTERS OR SYNTHESIZERS.

SIENNA: MUSIC HAS HEALING POWER. IT HAS THE ABILITY TO TAKE PEOPLE OUT OF THEMSELVES FOR A FEW HOURS.

JESSE: WOW. EXACTLY. YOU'RE PRETTY SMART.

SIENNA: ACTUALLY THAT WAS AN ELTON JOHN QUOTE.

JESSE: HA! WELL AT LEAST YOU'RE HONEST.

SIENNA: MOST OF THE TIME. ☺

CHAPTER EIGHT

I'm not expecting Grace to ask me to hang out after school, so when she does so the following Monday, I don't have a good excuse ready. I end up saying yes when normally I would have just gone home. Maybe it's because this whole Sienna thing has me thinking about making friends and Owen's been busy at soccer practice. Or maybe it's because I'm still not sure what I'm going to say in the Lexi video and doing something to get my mind off it for a while might help. Anyway, I end up at a construction site with a paintbrush in one hand and a cookie in the other. And, even though I'm not usually an oatmeal raisin fan, Grace has once again outdone herself. They are delicious.

The new Habitat for Humanity house is getting the last few touches put on it. Grace tells me she and her parents hope to turn it over to the new homeowners in just a few weeks. Inside, workers are finishing the flooring and plastering walls. Outside, Grace and I paint the front siding a cheery sky blue. Even with the constant noise of the banging and pounding, there is something soothing about covering a huge blank space with color. I love the way the paint soaks into the wood softly from the first swipe of the brush. Then the siding succumbs to the bright hue on the second pass. It makes me feel calmer than I have in weeks.

Grace dips her paintbrush in the bucket and makes one long stroke down the wood. She has a pink bandanna tied over her hair and a smudge of blue paint on one cheek. "So how's it going with Jesse?" she asks, cocking her head to one side and studying me.

My hand freezes. I panic. *Does Grace know about Sienna?* "What have you heard?"

"Nothing. Honestly. Just wondered how you were feeling about things."

"What *things*? You mean in chemistry?" Grace can't possibly have Spidey senses online, too.

Grace laughs. "Where else?"

I stuff a cookie in my mouth and chew, trying to give myself time to think. It's hard to swallow.

"I'm surviving," I say finally.

"Sometimes that's the best thing you can do," Grace says quietly. Her brush stills in midair. After a minute, she says, "There was this guy at my old school who was such a bully I had to leave."

I had no idea. "That's why you came to public school?"
Grace nods.

"But wasn't your old school a Christian school?"

She nods again and blinks a little harder than normal. *Is Grace going to cry?*

"There are bullies everywhere. Even places where they shouldn't be." Her voice is soft. "At first it was about silly stuff. My hair was too curly. My clothes were out of style. I talked too much."

The brush in Grace's hand trembles ever so slightly. I wait for her to go on.

"It was constant. It never stopped," Grace says. "And then it got worse. More physical. He started tripping me every time I walked down the hall and started throwing things at me behind the teachers' backs. Other people started laughing and that just encouraged him to do it more."

"Did you tell someone?"

"I tried. They said I should ignore him and he'd stop."

"But he didn't," I say.

"No." She shakes her head. "Sometimes I think I was a coward for leaving. I should have stood up to him instead of running away."

I mull this over, then say, "I guess Jesse's silly stunt with the Froot Loops in my locker sounded pretty trivial to you."

Grace meets my gaze. "Not at all. It's not what he did, but how it made you feel."

I don't understand. "But you told me to get over my feelings about Jesse!"

"I said to let it go for your own sake, not for his. But you're right. I shouldn't have said that. I'm sorry."

"Why did you say it, then?" I ask.

"That's what everyone told me when the bullying happened to me. Forgive and forget." She frowns. "I want it to be possible—the simple, right answer—but saying it doesn't make it so. I think something must be wrong with me because I couldn't do it for myself. But maybe you can."

"You haven't forgotten?" I ask.

She shakes her head fervently. "Never."

Her words make me shiver. Make me see Grace in a different way—and Sienna, too. Maybe Sienna isn't just about me and Jesse Santos. Maybe she's bigger than that. Maybe she can be a defender for all the bullied people. Like Grace. My resolve to make Sienna even more real hardens in my chest.

"Are you happier now?" I ask Grace.

"Oh my gosh, yes. A million times yes." Grace beams at me. "You and Owen are the best friends I've ever had."

Me? I don't know what to say.

Before I know what's happening, she closes the gap between us and hugs me. I don't hug back, but she doesn't seem to notice how stiffly my arms hang at my sides. Finally, I pat her back awkwardly to let her know she should let me go now, but she keeps hugging.

When Grace lets me go, she says, "I was thinking. We should go to homecoming together."

"You and Owen?" I ask.

"And you," she says. She dips the paintbrush back down in the paint.

I'm confused. "Don't you think that seems a little . . . crowded?"

"Absolutely not. It sounds like fun!"

I don't know if Owen will feel the same way. "I'll think about it."

We paint the rest of the wall without talking, accompanied by the bang of hammers and the carpenter's radio inside playing polka music loudly. I don't think about homecoming or Jesse or Sienna. I just think about color and the way the sun lightens the drying paint into an even more satisfying hue.

When I take my second cookie break, I watch two little girls playing out on the new driveway. The bigger of the two has a huge frown on her face and her hands placed firmly on her chubby hips. Her T-shirt is just a size too small and her jeans a size too large, but it is very clear she is the boss. A smaller version of her is scribbling furiously on the concrete with a big chunk of yellow sidewalk chalk. Every so often the younger girl looks up for approval, but the expression of the older girl standing over her doesn't budge. Evidently it isn't going so well.

"That driveway was just finished last week. Aren't you going to tell them to leave it alone?" I ask Grace, nodding toward the two kids.

"Why?" Grace asks. "It's their house. Or will be when we finish."

"Where are they living now?"

Grace motions with her chin toward the street, her hands still painting. "In that Dodge Caravan parked over there."

The old gray van looks like it's been in a few scrapes over the years. It sits unassuming at the curb, surrounded by modest newer homes and well-manicured front lawns. I feel something drop inside me. How many kids are living in cars in our sweet little town? I turn back to my job, but my mind is still on the girls in the driveway. Blue is a good color for this house, I think, brushing smooth some drips of paint from under a shingle. It is a color that symbolizes loyalty, strength, and wisdom. I hope for all of that for this new home.

Grace disappears inside to take cookies to the rest of the workers. Suddenly, the younger girl drops the chalk on the sidewalk and storms off toward the van, obviously frustrated with her opinionated older sister. The bossy girl shrugs and, to my surprise, heads in my direction.

She marches right up to me and folds her arms tightly over her chest. I go back to painting, ignoring her, but she doesn't budge. I can feel her staring at me.

I glance over my shoulder. "Do you want a cookie?" I ask.

The girl shakes her head, but keeps standing there staring at me. Little kids sometimes make me uncomfortable. They blurt out observations about my size in ways that are brutally honest.

"So what do you want?" I finally ask her.

"I want to draw a cat." Her voice is softer than I expected.

I turn around and look down at her. Her round white face is speckled with freckles and her eyes are as blue as the paint on my brush. "So do it," I tell her.

She shakes her head firmly. "I can't."

"But you haven't even tried." The words make an oddly significant echo in my brain. *Am I giving myself advice here?* I put the paint can down, balance the brush on top, and then walk over to look at the scrawls on the concrete. The girl follows me.

"My sister couldn't do it either," she explains.

"You're right," I say, and she nods in agreement. I think she's probably used to being right.

"Why a cat?" I ask her.

"My mom says we can get a cat when the house is finished. I want to draw a picture so he feels welcome coming home here."

I nod solemnly. It's the most logical reason I've ever heard for drawing a cat.

She holds the chalk out to me. "You draw it."

I start to say no, but the look on her face is enough to convince me. She's not going to take no for an answer. I squat down in the driveway and start to draw.

"Make it a very happy cat." She sits down beside me, cross-legged.

As I draw, I think about Katy Purry's soft black fur and white-tipped nose. I think about the way her tail twitches when she watches the birds outside the window. And I think about her rumbly purrs of delight when her favorite human, Veronica, holds her in her lap. My hand moves quickly across the surface of the driveway. I finish the face with a flourish of whiskers, then sit back on my knees to survey my work.

"Wow," she says reverently.

I glance over at the girl. She claps her hands together enthusiastically. I do a little fake bow and she claps harder.

"I didn't even know you had a happy cat inside you," she says incredulously.

"Me neither," I say with a smile.

CHITCHAT DIRECT MESSAGE

JESSE: HI CUTIE! HOW'S YOUR NIGHT GOING?

SIENNA: BETTER NOW. ☺

JESSE: I ASKED THE COACH ABOUT BEING IN THE HALFTIME SHOW.

SIENNA: WHAT DID HE SAY?

JESSE: HE LAUGHED.

SIENNA: IN A GOOD WAY?

JESSE: NOT REALLY BUT WE'LL SEE WHAT HAPPENS.

SIENNA: BUT YOU DID IT! GOOD FOR YOU.

JESSE: I NEVER WOULD HAVE DONE IT WITHOUT YOUR ENCOURAGEMENT. YOU'RE A GREAT PROBLEM SOLVER.

SIENNA: THANKS.

JESSE: DO YOU HAVE ANY PROBLEMS YOU NEED ADVICE ON? ☺

SIENNA: NAH, I'M GOOD.

JESSE: DO U GET ALONG WITH YOUR PARENTS?

JESSE: SORRY. WAS THAT TOO PERSONAL?

SIENNA: NO, IT'S FINE.

JESSE: OK WHEW.

SIENNA: AND YEAH, MOSTLY I DO. THEY KIND OF LET ME DO MY OWN THING. SOMETIMES, THEY FIGHT WITH EACH OTHER, BUT NOTHING TOO BAD.

JESSE: YOU'RE LUCKY.

SIENNA: DO UR PARENTS FIGHT?

JESSE: NOT ANYMORE.

SIENNA: THAT'S GOOD.

JESSE: NOT REALLY. THEY DIVORCED THREE YEARS AGO.

SIENNA: OH. SORRY.

JESSE: NO. IT'S BETTER. TRUST ME.

SIENNA: THANKS FOR BEING SO OPEN.

JESSE: NP.

SIENNA: I REALLY LIKE GETTING TO KNOW YOU. SEEING YOUR NAME POP UP ON MY SCREEN MAKES ME SMILE.

JESSE: ☺

JESSE: YOU LIVE IN DENVER, RIGHT?

SIENNA: YEAH.

JESSE: EVER COME TO FORT COLLINS?

SIENNA: I GOTTA GO. MY MOM'S TELLING ME TO TURN OFF THE LIGHTS.

JESSE: K. HAVE A GOOD NIGHT.

CHAPTER NINE

I can't sleep. The conversation with Jesse feels like a dream that can't be forgotten. But, the truth is, I don't want to let it go. I wonder for a minute if this is how werewolves feel after the full moon, when they've fully transformed.

I get out of bed and walk out into the hallway. My parents are in their room down the hall. I hear my dad snoring. I never knew Jesse's parents were divorced. I assumed everything about his life was perfect. And was he going to ask to meet in real life? I had to shut the conversation down, and fast. I'm not ready for that yet.

In the bathroom, I scrub my face without raising my eyes to look in the mirror. I don't want to see my reflection, but it has to happen eventually. When I lift my head, my round face and dark eyes stare back at me.

There is no sign of Sienna now, but she is inside me. I can feel her. Hear her. But there is still nothing of her in the mirror. I brush out my hair, impatiently and aggressively. Then I turn to go.

I head to Veronica's room. I open my sister's door and then close it behind me before I turn on the light. Compared to mine, her room is bland. Beige walls, navy-blue bedspread. Neat and tidy. It hasn't changed since she left. But the difference in our rooms is not just about color. I pick up a picture frame off her desk. It's of her and three of her best friends. On the wall are more photos. Every picture crowded with smiling faces. Volleyball teammates. Science fair project winners. Swim parties. Dances. But even with all the friends in her life, Veronica still made me feel special. That is her superpower.

I wish she were here with me, sitting on her bed with that half smile of hers. Ready to muss up my hair because it always made me crazy. Ready to laugh at some story I told her from school or to rehash a plotline from my favorite comic. I don't remember a time in my life without V in the room down the hall.

Enough is enough. I sit on her bed and pull out my phone to make a FaceTime call.

Veronica answers almost immediately. I instantly feel my features relax into a smile as her face pops into view. As usual, her light brown skin is clear and makeup-free except for a couple swipes of mascara. Her thick black hair is cut into a shaggy shoulder-length style that accentuates her high cheekbones. She's wearing a floral top I recognize as one of her go-to favorites. Our smiles are almost identical, but my face is rounder, my cheekbones less defined.

"Hey, Maisie. What's up?" I can barely hear her with all the music and noise in the background. She's in a restaurant, I can see.

"You're out," I say. "I can call back tomorrow."

"No, that's okay. It's just me and Paul." Her boyfriend, Paul, pops his head into view and gives me a goofy grin. Paul is a tall guy with a scruffy beard, wearing a blue stocking cap that almost perfectly matches his blue eyes. They started dating in Veronica's senior year in high school and both decided to go to California together for college.

He waves at me. "Hi, Maisie."

I hold a hand up. "Hey."

Paul is great. I like Paul. I just don't want to talk to Paul. I want to talk to my sister. Maybe she won't approve of Sienna, but at least I will have told someone what I've done and can explain it to the one person who might actually understand why I did it.

"We're eating sushi." Veronica makes an exaggerated happy face because she knows how much I hate sushi. She carefully props up the phone on something at the table so I can see both of them eating. It's almost like I'm sitting on the chair across from them.

"Wish you were here," Paul says. The dark stubble on his face and his thick black eyebrows only make his eyes more striking.

I wish I were there, too. Even with all the raw fish sitting around on little strips of rice.

Veronica picks up a piece of roll with her chopsticks and dips it into a bowl of wasabi. "Everything okay?" she asks.

"Yeah," I say, leaning back against the headboard. Maybe I can still tell her somehow even with the noise and Paul and the sushi. "Everything's good here."

I watch her pop the circle of rice into her mouth and chew. "How's school?" She talks with her mouth full.

I shrug. "Like always."

There's some commotion in the background and she looks over her shoulder toward something I can't see. When she looks back, she says, "This place is packed. Top spot in town for sushi. We had to wait forty-five minutes to get a seat."

"So I should let you go," I say, giving up on the idea of the big conversation.

"You sure you're okay?" she asks, knowing I'm not.

I nod, wanting to add *I miss you*, but Paul's right there and it feels stupid. Instead I say, "I'll talk to you tomorrow."

Paul pops his head back in to wave good-bye, then the screen goes black. I close my eyes and breathe in and out. When I open my eyes again, I look around the room, wishing again for V to be here. She seems so far away, physically and emotionally.

I pull myself up off the bed and go over to V's closet, sliding the door open. Just smelling the hint of her favorite citrus shower gel lingering on her left-behind clothes makes her feel closer. I pull out a navy top covered in a tiny print of rust-colored elephants. Holding it up to my chest, I know I can fit into the trapeze high-low style, but the color would be so different from my usual black uniform.

Sienna would wear this.

For a moment, all I can think about is how things would be different if I were Sienna. Not inside. Inside I'd still be me. But on the outside I'd be her. How would my life be now? I grieve for what could have been. I missed out on so many opportunities by my own choice—swimming parties, hikes, dances. Friends. Even what I wear—a black uniform of invisibility—is decreed by my outer appearance.

The grief bleeds into anger. Sienna isn't just for me, I remind myself. She represents every girl who's trained herself that being *good* at being fat means avoiding every possibility for criticism. She's for girls who've been bullied, or even just tossed aside by guys like Jesse. Maybe those other girls don't know how to shape-shift. But I do.

I yank the elephant top out of the closet and bring it with me into my room. It's a risky reminder of Sienna that I vow to wear to school tomorrow. It isn't a superhero costume, but it's a start. I lay the shirt out on my chair and sit down cross-legged on my carpet next to my bed. Beside me is a piece of paper I brought home from school—the permission slip for the Lexi Singh video audition. Am I really going to do this?

There is a knock on the door. My mom opens it slowly. "Want some company?" she asks softly.

I nod. She comes in. Katy Purry slips in behind her and they both join me on the floor. Mom and I lean back against the bed, our legs stretched out in front of us. Katy Purry curls into a ball between my feet.

"Did I hear you on the phone with your sister?" Mom asks.

"Yes," I say. "She was busy."

Mom pats my pajama-covered thigh but doesn't say anything.

"It's never going to be the same," I say quietly.

"No, it isn't," she agrees. "Veronica isn't always going to be down the hall, but she will always be your sister. No matter how far away you get." Mom looks at the paper beside me on the floor. "What's this?"

"It's a permission slip to apply to meet Lexi Singh. She's going to meet with some students for homecoming. Sort of a mentoring thing."

My mom nods. "I just read about it in the Parent Newsletter. You're going to apply, right?"

"I don't know. Maybe." I bite the inside of my lip and stare down at the carpet. "It's all on ChitChat and I'm not great on video."

Mom looks sideways at me. There is a silence between us while we both think. She reaches over and picks up the paper from the floor. "Why don't I sign this now and it will be ready when you decide?"

I smile and lean against her, putting my head down on her shoulder. She wraps her arm around me and brushes my hair back from my forehead. I think again about telling my mom about creating Sienna, but I know she wouldn't understand. And now I'm glad I didn't say anything to Veronica either.

It's wrong. I know it. But I'm still going to keep doing it. At least for now.

My mom signs the form and hands it to me. She studies my profile for a long minute, and then she says, "Do you know what?"

I glance at her. "What?"

"I could have almost been your twin when I was your age. We look so much alike."

I realize I've never seen pictures of my mom at my age. Older and younger, but not at sixteen. "Seriously?"

She nods.

"Did you ever want to look . . . different?" I ask.

She laughs. "Of course I did. Doesn't everyone at some point?"

I think about Jesse Santos. Maybe not everyone.

"I wanted to look just like a girl in my class. Her name was Katherine Dutton. No. I wanted to *be* Katherine." Mom gets a dreamy look in her eyes. "Everything about her was so perfect in every way. She was blonde and tiny and beautiful and popular."

I figure there is a moral coming at the end of this story, so I try to jump straight to it. "And she was ugly on the inside and her whole life turned out miserable after high school."

Mom shakes her head with a wry smile. "Hardly. I'm friends with her on Facebook. Looks like she is doing great. Her husband is an architect. The daughter goes to medical school. Her son is a star tennis player at the private school he attends. They vacation in Portugal. And Jamaica. There are check-ins at a winery in Napa and a Michelin-starred restaurant in New York."

"So what's your point?" I ask, because none of this sounds bad to me.

"My point is I wouldn't trade anything—not my looks or my life—for Katherine now. I am who I am supposed to be," she says. "Inside and out. And you are, too. But we become something special *because* of everything we are, not in spite of it."

Mom leans over to kiss my forehead, then tells me good night and slips out of my room. Katy Purry follows after her, and I stay sitting on the floor, holding the signed permission slip.

I don't feel special, but I feel better.

CHITCHAT DIRECT MESSAGE

DEZIREA: HEY. LOOKS LIKE WE HAVE SOME FOLLOWERS IN COMMON. HOW COME WE NEVER MET?

SIENNA: I LIVE IN DENVER.

DEZIREA: YOU ARE ADORBS! THAT'S ONLY AN HOUR AWAY. WE SHOULD TOTALLY HANG OUT SOMETIME. DO YOU EVER COME UP TO FORT COLLINS?

SIENNA: SURE. I'll DM YOU.

DEZIREA: COOL.

CHAPTER TEN

My dad's knock interrupts my chat with Dezirea.

"Maisie? Are you awake?" He opens the door a crack and sticks his head inside. "I'm leaving for the office."

I drag myself out of bed slowly, putting the computer on the nightstand. Last night Camila followed me on ChitChat and this morning Dezirea messaged me. Sienna is slowly coming into clearer view.

I use my curling iron to add in beachy waves to my long dark hair and apply a coat of mascara—more effort than I usually spend on my appearance. Before I can lose my nerve, I put on V's elephant blouse over a pair of skinny jeans. Then I add a black hoodie, but leave it unzipped.

Downstairs, I pop a bagel in the toaster, then pour Meow Mix into Katy Purry's empty bowl. She looks at me as though it is incredibly demeaning to have to eat such slop, but then puts her furry head halfway into the bowl and starts crunching away. I stifle a yawn, blink, and force my eyelids to stay open. The bagel pops out and I jump. I smear on some strawberry jelly and sit at the table alone, chewing and staring into space. My brain refuses to engage with reality. On the third bite, everything kicks in with a vengeance—filling my head with a long list of things I need to accomplish today.

I need to figure out what I'm going to do for the Lexi Singh video. And I need to reply to more ChitChat accounts to keep Sienna alive.

And I need more information from Jesse.

"Hi, sweetie." My mom comes down the stairs with a coffee cup in one hand and her phone in the other. "You look cute."

"Thanks," I mumble through my last bite of bagel.

She glances down at her phone. "Oh, that's cool," she comments.

"What?" I ask, picking up my plate to take it to the dishwasher.

"My colleague from Denver is thinking about moving up here. She has a daughter about your age."

I nod, my mind still on my to-do list.

"I should introduce the two of you."

I stand up and rinse off the knife in the sink.

"Her name is Claire."

My hand freezes, the water still running over the knife and into the sink. *No. It can't be.* The girl whose image I used to become Sienna? I remember that I saw her picture on a profile connected to my mom. But still. What would be the chances that Mom is referring to that same girl? There must be a million other Claires. Right?

My mom reaches around me and turns off the water. "You better hurry. You're going to be late."

Owen and I pull into a parking space in the student lot. Outside of the school, groups of kids hang out. Some gather on the benches. Some sit on the concrete ledge that lines the walkway leading to the front doors. There's even a large group sitting in a circle out on the grass. It doesn't look like some picturesque high school movie to me. It feels like the start to a horror movie. The elephant shirt I'm wearing is such a tiny change. When I left home a few minutes ago, it felt like a good one. Now I'm not so sure.

"We should go in," Owen tells me from the passenger seat.

"One second," I say. I twist the rearview mirror toward me and apply one coat of MAC Russian Red lipstick for courage. Owen watches me, puzzled. He's not used to seeing me put on makeup.

Then I grab my backpack from the back seat of the Jeep Wrangler, and open the car door.

Outside, the wind whips my hair across my face as I struggle to get out. The gust is so powerful it pushes back against the door, making it almost impossible to open. Finally, I make it outside and slam the door with more force than necessary.

Showtime.

Owen and I walk to the school entrance together. The wind blows the colors of fall across the still-green grass, mussing girls' hair and tossing about discarded pieces of notebook paper. My eyes focus on the tree beside the front doors and one red leaf fluttering wildly at the very top. There is something sad about the way that one leaf clings so determinedly to the top branch, even though everyone knows the coming winter will be its downfall. I want to be as determined and undaunted as that leaf.

Inside the school, Owen heads for the boys' bathroom, and I continue on to my locker. I pull out my books for class and hang up my hoodie inside, my heart pounding. When I close my locker door and step away, I come face-to-face with Bella and Hunter going toward their lockers at the end of the hall.

I don't move. My stomach clenches.

"Oh, look. The elephant is wearing elephants. How appropriate," Hunter says in a loud stage whisper I am meant to hear.

A deep flush of embarrassment crawls from my stomach to my cheeks.

Bella laughs. "Excuse us," she says to me in a singsong voice.

Sienna wouldn't move. Something hardens inside my chest and I like it.

"Go around me," I say.

"Are you kidding me?" Hunter asks.

I cross my arms in front of my chest and step in even closer. "Does it look like I'm kidding?"

There is surprise in his eyes, then a small glint of something that looks almost like fear. Bella grabs his arm and pulls him to the side.

"It's not worth it," Bella whispers. "She's crazy."

Maybe I am.

I stand there long after they leave, breathing hard, the satisfaction pulsing through my brain. When I feel a hand on my shoulder, I turn to find Owen standing beside me. "What do cows like to do at a concert?" he asks.

I don't say anything. My mind is still on my tiny victory over Bella and Hunter. *Not now, Owen.*

"Make *mooo*sic," he says. He half smiles.

"Why is this joke thing so important to you?" I ask sharply. My patience with his new obsession is running out. *Can't we just be like everybody else? Even just a little bit?*

Owen shrugs. He has a confused look on his face, and I instantly feel guilty.

"Everybody needs a little silliness in their lives. Why can't it come from me? Is that so bad?" he asks quietly.

"Don't you care that people think you're weird?"

He stares at the floor and shoves his hands in his pockets. "Do *you* think I'm weird?"

Seeing his face, something twists in my heart. My mood isn't Owen's fault.

"Absolutely."

Finally, he looks up at me, eyes locked on mine like we're the only ones in the crowded hallway. "Oh, thank God," he mumbles fervently.

I laugh.

"Because I would never want to be like Hunter and his crowd," he adds.

"You heard?" I ask.

"We don't have the energy to worry about people like that," he says. "That's what I've always admired about you."

Trying to smile, I touch his arm. "And that's why we'll always be best friends. Even if your jokes aren't funny."

He holds up a hand to his forehead and makes a mock salute. "Froot Loops forever."

I mimic his movement. "Froot Loops forever!"

              ⌗   ⌗   ⌗

When we get to chemistry, Jesse is already there. He's been busy. Just not in relation to anything useful or remotely related to our actual assignment. He's in his seat and zoned out, listening to music on his earbuds as usual. But a piece of paper is on the table in front of my stool.

Apparently, Jesse did his own sketch. It is a stick figure with a huge head. Above it he drew a word bubble that says, *"I am obviously the smartest person in the world."* The word *obviously* has three black lines drawn under it for emphasis. The stick figure has long dark hair and a T-shirt on that says *"Froot Loop."* Like I didn't know it was supposed to be me. My face burns. At least he didn't try and draw my body.

He pulls his headphones out of his ears and I hear the sound of some kind of jazz music playing loudly before he clicks the phone to silence. He grins, making that dimple appear again in his left cheek. "Do you like your portrait?"

"You're very talented." I will not let him see that his stupid little sketch got under my skin.

"Well, I know you like to draw. And since I think you really ARE the smartest person in the world . . ."

"Obviously," I say. My eyebrows rise. There is an ask coming. I can feel it. But if this is Jesse's way of trying to get something from me, he's not very good at it.

"So, I need a favor."

"Of course you do."

"I was thinking maybe you could help me with this big lab write-up?"

The lab write-up is our main assignment for the semester. Mr. Vance gave us worksheets for it, and we're supposed to start work on it today.

"You mean do it for you?" I sweep the drawing off to the side and sit down on my stool.

"No, I mean *help* me. I'll do my part. Promise." He holds up his hand like he's swearing on the Bible in a court of law. The well-practiced flirt comes back into his voice even though it's completely wasted on me. He just can't stop. I can feel my mood starting to shift. Jesse Santos needs *me*. I feel a certain sense of control.

I scowl at him. *Game on.*

He says, "You know, you look prettier when you smile."

Ugh. And just like that, he reverts back to his usual, obnoxious self.

"I smile," I reply sharply. "Just not at you."

"Why not?" He sounds hurt.

"Because you draw mean pictures and make fun of me."

"That?" He motions toward the picture. "It was just a stupid joke. Because you're good at drawing and I'm really bad at it and . . . I thought it might make you laugh."

There might have actually been a compliment buried in there somewhere?

"It didn't."

"I can see that now." He leans back on his stool, his arms crossed, his gaze focused on the ceiling.

I ask, "Do you want to pass this class or not?"

He looks at me. All the fake, put-on smolder is gone. "I don't want to pass it. I *have* to."

"Then let's get to work."

He wraps his earbuds up carefully and puts them in a special zipper case, then back in his backpack.

"What were you listening to?" I ask, remembering suddenly that I need more information for Sienna.

"Steve Coleman and Five Elements."

"Who?"

He stares smugly at me, his thick eyebrows raised. "Only one of the best jazz saxophonists you can ever see live."

I shrug. "Never heard of him."

"Not surprised," he says. "But to be fair, most people in this room haven't."

And there's the attitude again. I make a vow to listen to as many Steve Coleman songs as I can get my hands on.

"Enough of this fun stuff," he says. "What do we do first?"

I shove the lab worksheet across the table at him. "Read it."

Jesse sits up straighter, a frown of concentration crossing his face. "Use the equipment you have available to make observations of the components and determine their properties," he reads aloud. He looks at the box of materials in front of us. "So what do we have available?"

"These four substances." I take each item out of the material box one by one. "And a hot plate, paper towels, can lid, and a Sharpie."

We spend the rest of the time trying to figure out the melting point for four solids—dextrose, wax, sugar, and salt. According to Mr. Vance, the lab will help us apply the concepts from his last lecture on bonding and intermolecular forces.

When we finish, I say, "Okay. Shock me. Say something intelligent."

"You're on," Jesse says. He opens his notebook and reads aloud from his class notes: "At the melting point, particles that are in a specific solid structural arrangement gain more motional freedom without changing chemical composition."

"Aww. It's so cute when you try to talk about things you don't understand."

He just laughs. "And that's exactly why you're here."

"So tell me what that means in your own words," I say.

"Basically, things can change shape, but they are still the same thing. Inside. Where it counts."

The truth of his statement sucks the breath out of me. "Do you believe that?" I manage to ask.

He looks at me for a moment, then taps the notebook in front of us. "Of course I do. That's exactly what we just proved in our lab. Science doesn't lie."

But I do.

"So we have to find the time to work on this lab write-up," I say. "We could split things up. Do you want to do the procedure and I'll do the conclusion?"

Jesse shakes his head. He fills the dropper up with the liquid from the beaker. "I can't risk screwing this up. I need your help."

I can tell it's killing him to admit it. A little smile forms on my lips.

"Okay. How about Saturday?" I offer. The thought of spending time with Jesse outside of class is stressful, but we don't have much of a choice. Not if we want to pass this assignment.

"I can't," he says. "Football game. It's an away game. I won't be home until late."

I sigh. "You have to give somewhere." I check the calendar on my phone. "What about Sunday afternoon? Three o'clock?"

"Can't," he says firmly, shaking his head. "I have a standing appointment."

I look at him incredulously. "On Sunday afternoon? For what?"

Jesse looks away, frowning. He's hiding something. What does he do every Sunday afternoon? Maybe there is a mystery girl somewhere. Maybe Sienna can get to the bottom of that.

Eventually he sighs. "I just can't do it at three."

The bell rings. I shrug, then stand up and pick up my book bag. "Okay, but if this is important to you, you'll have to make time for it."

I don't get halfway to the door before he stops me. "Maisie. Wait."

I turn and look at him, raising an eyebrow.

"What about earlier on Sunday? We could meet at the downtown library?"

I don't have the energy to argue with him. "Okay," I say finally, turning back toward the door.

"So Sunday, then? One o'clock?" I can hear the grin in his voice. I put my thumb up over my shoulder on the way out the door.

CHITCHAT DIRECT MESSAGE

JESSE: HOW'S YOUR DAY GOING? AM BORED AT LUNCH.

SIENNA: HA. SAME.

JESSE: CAN I TELL YOU SOMETHING?

SIENNA: ?

JESSE: I CAN'T STOP THINKING ABOUT YOU.

SIENNA: WHY? YOU DON'T EVEN KNOW ME.

JESSE: THEN LET'S DO IT.

SIENNA: WHAT?

JESSE: LET'S GET TO KNOW EACH OTHER. FAVORITE COLOR?

SIENNA: THE COLOR OF A MERMAID'S TAIL.

JESSE: IS THAT GREEN OR BLUE?

SIENNA: MORE GREEN. YOU?

JESSE: THE BLUE OF THE SKY RIGHT AFTER SUNSET. IT'S NOT GOING TO LAST. IF YOU DON'T NOTICE IT, YOU'LL MISS IT.

SIENNA: THAT'S A GOOD ONE.

JESSE: THANKS. FAVORITE SMELL?

SIENNA: BACON. DEFINITELY BACON. YOU?

JESSE: BABIES.

SIENNA: ???? WHY?

JESSE: I VOLUNTEER AT THE HOSPITAL ON SUNDAYS IN THE PREEMIE WARD. IT'S MY HAPPY PLACE.

SIENNA: REALLY?

JESSE: YEP. MY MOM IS A NURSE SO SHE GOT ME STARTED ON THAT.

SIENNA: COOL.

JESSE: YOUR TURN TO ASK A QUESTION.

SIENNA: OK. FAVORITE FOOD?

JESSE: PROMISE YOU WON'T LAUGH?

SIENNA: NO.

JESSE: PURPLE PEEPS.

SIENNA: . . .

JESSE: YOU'RE LAUGHING, AREN'T YOU?

SIENNA: MORE LIKE GAGGING.

SIENNA: WAIT. DO THEY HAVE TO BE PURPLE??

JESSE: ABSOLUTELY.

JESSE: ← BIG FAN OF THE EASTER BUNNY.

SIENNA: NOW I'M LAUGHING.

JESSE: WHAT'S YOUR FAVORITE FOOD?

SIENNA: CHICKEN ADOB

SIENNA: . . . I MEAN CHICKEN.

JESSE: CHICKEN?

SIENNA: YEAH.

JESSE: ALL KINDS? ☺

SIENNA: YEP.

JESSE: MAYBE WE CAN GO OUT FOR CHICKEN AND PURPLE PEEPS SOMETIME.

SIENNA: SOUNDS FUN. OOPS THE LUNCH BELL IS RINGING. GOT TO GO.

CHAPTER ELEVEN

Owen has soccer practice after school, but he texts me to meet him at Old Firehouse Books. I love this place. It's tucked away inside a historic redbrick building across from the town square.

I nod at the woman behind the counter on my way into the store. My thoughts are still on Sienna's latest ChitChat with Jesse, and all she—and I—learned about him. None of it adds up with the Jesse I know. I have to get my mind off of him and Sienna for a while.

I don't slow down to look at the greeting cards or T-shirts. The walls are crowded with books, and I make my way through the narrow aisles that lead to the children's section in the back. In an arched opening between the two sections, I grab a reading chair and make myself comfortable with one of Lexi Singh's latest graphic novels and my sketchpad. Within minutes, I immerse myself in Lexi's world, my own notebook lying open and blank in my lap.

I pull out of my Lexi trance about thirty minutes later with the realization that Owen is late. He is never late. It makes me nervous, and suddenly not even Nosy Parker's newest adventures can keep my concentration. I pull out my phone and text him.

ME: WHERE ARE YOU?

OWEN: AT PALMER'S FLOWER SHOP

ME: WHY?

OWEN: WILL EXPLAIN. ON MY WAY NOW.

When Owen finally arrives, he has a bouquet of red and yellow zinnias wrapped in brown paper and tied with a string.

Stranger and stranger.

The first thing out of his mouth is "You see any new joke books?"

I relax, thinking that some things have not changed.

"I wasn't looking for them," I say, staring pointedly at the flowers.

He ignores my obvious question. "I'll look later. Let's go next door to Happy Lucky's Teahouse."

I raise my eyebrows. "You're not going to even look?"

"Not today."

Happy Lucky's connects to the bookstore through a side door beside the bestseller wall. I'm not a big fan of tea, but Owen went through a self-study of the history of tea some time ago and never went back to coffee or soft drinks. Today he immediately orders a Black Dragon oolong from the girl at the counter before she can even ask what he wants, which again seems off. Normally Owen would smell his way through all the green and black teas at least once, then carefully sip the samples on the small table by the door before finally making a decision. I order a French press coffee and earn a slightly disappointed frown from the cashier for not being a tea aficionado.

I grab an empty table in the front with a view of Walnut Street and the shops across the way. While I wait for Owen to finish paying, I watch the action across the street. A guy steps out of Spoons, the soup and salad place, with a big sack of takeout and quickly dodges a woman pushing a baby stroller with one hand and guiding a toddler with the other. A row of women sit in the window seats of the salon Studio Be, with foil-wrapped hair and black capes, waiting for the beautification magic to happen. Out on the street, a red SUV waits patiently for the first open parking spot.

My fingers tingle. I want to capture it all on paper—the normalcy of the scene would make a perfect backdrop for fantasy. I can imagine my main character striding along the sidewalk in all her superhero magnificence, her bright red cape flopping along in the wind behind her. She would stand out like a shining beacon of hope in an otherwise completely ordinary world. I can almost see the look of wonder on the toddler's face as he stares up at my caped crusader.

The idea of adding my bully-fighting superhero to this world starts the creative process going in my mind. I want more. Instead of the SUV waiting for a spot, I'd draw a dragon puffing smoke out its nose impatiently. And an assortment of peacocks would replace the women in the beauty shop chairs, their plumage decorated with tiny tinfoil hats. I smile. Maybe Lexi sat here one day in this very spot and created *her* world.

Owen appears, breaking into my thoughts. He carefully places the bouquet of flowers on the table, and we wait for our respective drinks to brew. I turn over the tiny hourglass provided and set it beside one of the bright yellow blooms.

"So." I watch Owen sniff at his steaming pot, and then ask, "What's up with the flowers?"

"They're for Grace." He pushes a stray curl out of one eye, looking eagerly at me. His intensity is laser-like. "Do you think she'll like them?"

"Sure. I guess so." I frown. There's a lot to take in here. Flowers? Does Owen *like* Grace? Seeing the earnest way he wants to please her makes me wish someone felt that way about me. It also makes me feel more than a little jealous. "Is she sick?"

"No. I just think they are . . ." He pauses, searching for the right word. "Cheerful."

"I guess so," I mutter. "If you like that kind of thing."

The day after the Froot Loops locker incident, Owen showed up at my house with a beautifully wrapped present. Inside was a hardback collection of *The Legend of Wonder Woman*, a digital-first series by Renae De Liz. It was wondrous, powerful, and inspiring. And somehow Owen knew it was exactly the right thing to put in my hands that day.

The last of the grains trickle into the bottom of the timer and I push the plunger down on my coffeepot.

"I was thinking you could help me," Owen says.

I pour the coffee into my cup and add a dose of cream, stirring the blackness into a rich brown. "With what?"

"I need some . . . relationship . . . advice." His voice sounds strange, high and wobbly.

My hand stops with my cup halfway to my mouth. *Relationship? Owen and Grace?* I never thought about Owen as being someone's boyfriend before.

There is a brief, thick silence. His tea sits untouched in front of him.

I take a sip and swallow. "What kind of relationship advice?"

"I was just wondering if *someone* wanted to go on a date, how they would ask . . . someone." He doesn't say her name, but we both know exactly who he is talking about. *Grace.* "Where would they go? That sort of thing."

I swallow hard. Owen looks down at the table and stops talking abruptly, messing with his tea bag. A red flush climbs up his neck and into his face.

I put my cup on the table, lean my head back against the wall, and look up at the ceiling. I feel him watching me. "And you're asking me for this advice?"

Owen nods.

I think about that kiss we shared years ago, under the mistletoe. *Did* Owen like me back then? I don't know. Maybe. But that was so long ago. And in the end, Owen and I were never going to work as anything more than best friends.

I put a hand out and touch his arm, forgetting for a moment his aversion to random touching. "First things first. Just relax. Ask her if she wants to hang out with you sometime."

"Wait." Owen holds up a hand to stop me from talking, then pulls out a yellow legal pad and pen from his backpack. He writes on the pad and I read it upside down. *Ask her to hang out.*

"Okay. What's next?" He cocks his head and looks at me expectantly. "What would *you* like to do on a first date?"

I realize I don't know that much about Grace other than she can be the most obnoxiously happy person on the planet. "I'm probably not the best person to ask."

He flinches, a worried little wrinkle between his eyes.

I can't avoid the conversation, even though it makes me uncomfortable. It's only going to frustrate him.

"Movies are never good for a first date. You can't really talk to each other," I say slowly. I swirl the spoon around in my coffee, letting myself dream for a minute about the idea. If I were wearing my Sienna disguise, there would be so many more options. I need to think more like her. "You could hike to the top of Horsetooth Rock and watch the sunset. Take a class together—pottery, maybe. Or cooking. I think there's a special cooking school at Ginger and Baker."

Corn maze. Farmers' market. Escape room. I start to feel the limits lift from my mind, imagining how fun all of it could be with the right person. But just as quickly, I shut it all down.

Owen thinks about it for a second, then looks pleased. "I like it. Anything else?"

I shoot him a sideways glance. Maybe Grace hasn't said anything to him about the three of us going to the homecoming dance together? "Well, if you want to go more traditional, there's obviously the big homecoming festivities coming up. Bonfire. Parade. Dance. Lots of opportunities there."

Meeting Lexi Singh, I think. Although that's not really a date idea.

He writes on the paper in front of him and I give him a thumbs-up when he looks up from the pad. He stretches out his long legs and stares at the toes of his sneakers. I wait. Owen finally pours his tea into the cup and asks, "But what if she says no?"

I roll my eyes. "Any girl who turns you down is a complete idiot," I say. "I hope you realize that."

He gives me a smile, his green eyes crinkling at the corners, and his face transforms. I think Owen and I are friends because of his smiles. Grace is a very lucky girl. I hope she knows that.

"I have a feeling you don't have to worry," I add, because who could possibly turn down the opportunity to have those smiles around all the time?

He changes the subject. "I think you should definitely submit an application video to meet Lexi."

"I was thinking about it, but . . ." My voice trails off, full of all my doubts and uncertainties.

"It's your big break. You can't pass up an opportunity like that!"

I mull this over a minute, then nod slowly. "It could work. But it's statistically improbable. There are going to be so many people like Dezirea and Camila trying to get in to meet her. I'm not sure I can put myself out there like that. And if I do somehow get to meet her, can I really show her my drawings?" I shudder.

"What's the worst that can happen?" Owen asks.

We both know what could happen. *Ridicule. Humiliation. Rejection.*

"I know it's a long shot, but you can do it," Owen says firmly. He truly believes it. I can tell. Strangely, it makes me feel calmer about the whole thing.

"It's a crazy idea," I say, then take another sip from my mug.

He smiles. "Crazy awesome," he agrees.

A movement at the window makes both of us look over. The woman with the baby carriage is outside looking in with a hand cupped around her face to block the glare.

"Move oolong," Owen says quietly. "Nothing to tea here."

I can't help but laugh.

Leaving the tea shop, I realize an idea for the video has started to form in my mind. I practically run toward my car, a new sense of confidence straightening my shoulders and filling my brain. I pass the mother again. The little boy holding her hand is about three, with blond curls and a wide smile. He looks at me, then starts singing loudly to his own made-up tune, "Big fat girl . . ."

The words sink in and stab me. Just by walking outside, by existing, I invite rude comments. This shell I wear makes me a target for the world to say rude things. How could I have forgotten? His mother grabs him by the shoulders. "Shush," she says urgently. She mumbles "Sorry" as they pass by.

My heart thudding in my chest, I stand, frozen, the heat rising up my neck like flames. They walk away, hand in hand. My high-waist skinny jeans with shredded rips seemed so fashionable a few hours before. They now feel like a tent. I tug my elephant shirt down over my thighs.

I'm not angry at the child. Or the mom. I'm angry at myself. On my best day, when I walk out of the house feeling my hair is perfect and my outfit is incredibly cool, I am still fat. The photos and videos and comments live to remind me. People feel like they have to tell me. Over and over again. Like I could possibly forget.

I've been fooling myself. Maybe Sienna isn't my superhero alter ego.

She is my escape.

CHITCHAT DIRECT MESSAGE

JESSE: HOW YA DOIN?

SIENNA: UGH. I'M IN A BAD MOOD.

JESSE: WHY?

SIENNA: MY BEST GUY FRIEND HAS A NEW GIRLFRIEND.

JESSE: IS THAT GOOD OR BAD?

SIENNA: IT'S GOOD. TOTALLY GOOD. I THINK IT'S
GOOD.

JESSE: WHY DO I THINK YOU'RE NOT TOO SURE ABOUT
THIS?

SIENNA: JUST BEING SELFISH.

JESSE: WHY?

SIENNA: I WILL MISS HIM.

JESSE: HE'S NOT GOING AWAY. EVERYBODY GETS NEW
FRIENDS. DOESN'T MEAN THEY LEAVE THE OLD ONES
HANGING.

SIENNA: I GUESS.

JESSE: DO YOU LIKE HER?

SIENNA: SHE'S NICE.

JESSE: "NICE" IS NOT A GREAT COMPLIMENT.

SIENNA: DO YOU HAVE A BEST FRIEND?

JESSE: I HAVE LOTS OF THEM.

SIENNA: THAT'S NOT HOW *BEST* FRIENDS WORK.

JESSE: THEN I'M DOING IT WRONG. TELL ME HOW TO BE A BEST FRIEND.

SIENNA: BEST FRIENDS KNOW YOUR BIGGEST DREAMS AND YOUR WORST FEARS.

JESSE: WHAT'S YOUR BIGGEST DREAM? *PRACTICING TO BECOME A BEST FRIEND*

SIENNA: . . .

JESSE: *WAITING.* BEST FRIENDS ARE VERY PATIENT.

SIENNA: I WANT TO BE A SUPERHERO.

JESSE: HA! NO, SERIOUSLY.

SIENNA: I AM SERIOUS.

JESSE: YOU ARE FREAKING WEIRD *IN A TOTALLY COOL WAY*

SIENNA: WHAT ABOUT YOU? WHAT'S UR BIG DREAM???

JESSE: TO PLAY MY OWN MUSIC FOR PEOPLE.

SIENNA: LOTS OF PEOPLE?

JESSE: I'D SETTLE FOR JUST ONE PERSON.

SIENNA: WHY DON'T YOU DO IT?

JESSE: HARD. SCARY. MIGHT SUCK BIG-TIME. MIGHT BE BAD. REALLY BAD.

SIENNA: THAT'S YOUR WORST FEAR, TOO?

JESSE: YEAH. YOU?

SIENNA: DISAPPEARING.

JESSE: SRSLY? LOOKING AT YOU, I'M PRETTY SURE PEOPLE WOULD NOTICE IF YOU WERE GONE.

SIENNA: ARE YOU OKAY IF WE ARE JUST FRIENDS ON HERE?

JESSE: TOTALLY.

SIENNA: I LIKE IT.

JESSE: ME TOO ☺

JESSE: BUT I COULD BE AN EVEN BETTER BEST FRIEND IN REAL LIFE!!

CHAPTER TWELVE

On Wednesday, everyone is talking about the Lexi Singh auditions. It's like a wildfire flickering down the halls and slipping up the walls. In every corner, in every hallway, at every locker, at every lunch table—someone is discussing what they are going to do for their ChitChat video. If they are lucky, a friend is listening to them practice their spiel aloud. Over and over again. Sure the video is supposed to *look* natural and unrehearsed, but no one is going to be crazy enough to actually freestyle it.

The electricity builds as the hours tick down to the beginning of the ChitChat air time. At five o'clock tonight it goes live. At eight o'clock it will be all over, and the window to Lexi will slam shut. The suspense is killing all of us.

Something of Sienna still lingers in my mind from my last exchange with Jesse. Or maybe it was reading the Wonder Woman book late into the night. Either way, I feel more confident and bolder than usual. I survived the elephant shirt, so now I'm ready to kick it up a notch. Everyone knows big girls aren't supposed to wear horizontal stripes or prints or bright colors, but today I wear what I want: a flowy chiffon maxi dress covered in pale pink flowers. I balance out all the pink with a black moto jacket and black, high-heeled ankle booties. My long dark hair is up in a messy bun at the nape of my neck and I wear a pair of sunglasses that, according to the CurvyFashionista ChitChat account I follow, go with the outfit perfectly.

Of course, I know the classroom rules, and the sunglasses will go in my backpack when the tardy bell rings. But for now, they are my favorite accessory—giving me a little dark distance from the surrounding judgment and helping me feel like a superhero in disguise as I walk down the hall toward chemistry and Jesse Santos.

Owen and Grace stand by the vending machines, waiting for me.

"Cool outfit," Grace says enthusiastically. Owen just raises his eyebrows.

Bella walks by wearing a tiny Mango buttoned denim skirt and a ribbed wool sweater that accentuates her curves. She glances toward me, her eyes widening, and then she does a double take. And not in a good way. I so wanted to believe *Teen Vogue* when they tweeted, *"Stop following the rules about what big girls aren't supposed to wear and feel free to experiment with different looks."* Only right now it feels like really terrible advice. Then I think, what would happen if I actually didn't care?

If I can't hide, I might as well give them something to stare at.

In chemistry, Jesse glances at my outfit, but thankfully doesn't say anything. I put the too-small lab apron on over my dress, but leave the ties dangling at my sides. Then I read the directions on the latest handout from Mr. Vance. "We're supposed to purify this mixture."

Jesse inspects the beaker. "It just looks like dirty water to me."

"There are four different elements in that water," I tell him. "And we need to describe how we're going to separate it into the four different components."

He tosses his goggles up in the air and then catches them, grinning at me. "No problem. I got this."

I don't smile back. He hasn't even looked at the directions. "You don't know what you're talking about."

"I think I do."

"I think you don't."

The smile disappears from his face and his eyes narrow. "Let me explain it to you in terms you can understand."

"I'm the one who doesn't understand?"

"Wait. Just listen." Jesse waves his hands. "This whole school is a mixture, but you can definitely separate the whole into individuals by knowing more about them."

My brows furrow. "What do you mean?"

"Okay. Dezirea is pretty popular, right?"

"Yeah." *Understatement.*

"And her whole crowd of friends is, too?"

I nod. *Including you.* "You're making it sound like popularity is a virtue."

"Who said *virtue*?" Jesse asks, shaking his head. "I didn't say it was a good thing."

"Fine," I huff. "Go on with your analogy."

Jesse nods. "So let's say Dezirea's crowd is iron. The next hottest thing will attract them just like a magnet."

"And they all stick together." I smile in spite of myself. "So if someone waved . . ." I think about the ChitChats of Dezirea's party. "Waved a party over them, all the iron would go out of the mixture?" I ask.

"Bam. Out of the mix," he agrees.

"Got it." I pick up the magnet and pull out the bits of iron from the mixture. Jesse supervises closely. "Okay," I say. "What . . . or who . . . is next?"

"Those little things floating on the top." He points.

I pick up a handheld magnifying glass and peer down at the beaker. "I think those are poppy seeds."

He nods. "Those are the super-smart kids. The innovators. The ones who float above all the high school drama and stay true to who they are."

I'm impressed. Who knew he'd be able to come up with something like that after looking at soggy seeds?

Jesse adds, "We need them."

But no one wants to be them.

Jesse points toward Owen with his thumb. "Take Froot Loop over there. He's going to change the world someday."

I'm surprised. *That's how he thinks of Owen?*

I take a sieve and scoop out all the poppy seeds until

there is nothing left floating in the mixture. It definitely looks less interesting.

Jesse picks up the beaker and holds it up to the light. "There's definitely still something in there." He swirls the liquid around a little more. "Maybe . . . salt?"

"How would we remove the salt from the mixture?" I'm testing him, but he knows the answer.

"We boil it out."

I turn on the hot plate and put the beaker on top, then ask, "So who in this mixed-up world of yours is salt?"

He gives me a one-shoulder shrug. Is Jesse Santos blushing? "There's a girl I talk to on ChitChat sometimes. She reminds me of salt. She adds flavor and interest to everything. Spices it up."

My head feels suddenly light and my heart starts hammering.

"Really?" I ask, trying hard to keep my face blank.

Something in Jesse's eyes shifts. He looks . . . happy. "Yeah. Just the little bit I know her makes things . . . better."

"Who is she?" I make myself ask.

"Actually, I haven't met her. She lives in Denver."

He's talking about me . . . *Sienna*. It feels like a fist to my stomach. The plan is working. I should feel a lot better about this than I do.

I change the subject.

"So we're still meeting on Sunday, right?" I know my voice sounds weird, but he doesn't seem to notice.

"Yep." He leans over the water and watches carefully as it begins to boil.

⇖ ⇖ ⇖

The Jesse/Sienna business distracts me from the Lexi Singh video for a short while, but now I'm in history class and the attention has shifted back to the most popular topic in school.

"What are you going to say in your video?" Camila asks Dezirea before class starts.

I pretend not to listen, focusing instead on Owen sitting at the desk in front of me. My pencil moves across the page, sketching quickly the lines of his shirt collar.

"I'm just going to introduce myself and talk about my interests," Dezirea says, shrugging.

I draw the way Owen's hair curls when it hits the nape of his neck.

Camila shrugs. "Okay. Whatever. I'm sure you will look great."

No, I think. *You will look fantastic.*

"You better believe it," Dezirea says. "We're stars in the making."

Camila laughs. "Tell me something I don't know."

I glance down at my desk and my eyes land on my own hand holding the pencil. I freeze, blinking, seeing myself with the same attention to detail as I was giving to my drawing. My fingers are short and stubby. I can't make myself look at my arm. I look back over at Dezirea and Camila.

"Okay, babe." Dezirea laughs. "You and me are set to totally crush this thing."

They high-five each other and my heart drops. How am I supposed to make a video of myself when I can't even look at my own arm? But I have to go through with this tonight. Even if it means going up against the popular crowd on ChitChat.

⌖ ⌖ ⌖

As soon as I get home from school, I practice my ChitChat video in front of the mirror and make myself watch it. My hair is a mess, so I brush it. My hands shake, so I sit on one to still it. My eyes are good, intense and full of passion. I focus on that. I feel the clock ticking down to five p.m. along with my pulse. Sort of like an explosive device counting down the seconds until detonation. Katy Purry sits on my bed looking at me with her usual bored expression. I realize she could destroy a live video, so it takes me almost ten minutes to catch her and put her outside in the hall. Now, when I don't want her around, she is suddenly my best friend.

I spend thirty minutes styling my hair. *Curls? No curls? Up? Down?* My makeup takes another half hour, with extra attention paid to a natural eye shadow palette and layered coats of mascara. Then, after a long time of staring at my closet, I finally decide on a sunflower print, Brigitte Bardot–inspired off-the-shoulder dress that

@CurvyFashionista said would make anyone feel like a 1950s screen goddess.

A final quick look in the mirror, then it's time. I log in to ChitChat. Lexi's people were smart enough to turn off the ability to comment on the live video feed, to try to prevent online trolls. With ChitChat live, it is impossible to know how many people actually view a video before it disappears into the vast blue internet.

Dezirea's video is live right now. She looks beautiful. Not surprising. I *am* surprised that she is wearing a simple black leotard and tights.

"My name is Dezirea Davis and I enjoy dancing, and hanging out with my friends. I am a huge fan and I would love the opportunity to meet you."

She backs away from the camera until her whole body is in frame. Then she spins ever so slowly, her leg extended and bent behind her and one arm held high. This is a totally different dancer than the Dezirea-as-cheerleader everyone knows. The one we've seen on the football field sidelines, shaking pom-poms to the fight song. Her athletic build is toned, definitely not the traditional ballerina body. I watch, mesmerized, and marvel at how strong she must be. Yet every movement, every turn, looks so easy and graceful. I don't realize I'm holding my breath until she stops and does a deep curtsy, head bowed.

I'm proud of her for showing this side of herself to the world. Maybe we're not that different. We both have sides we keep hidden from view, afraid others might crush our precious dreams. If things had turned out differently, maybe we would have encouraged each other more.

Camila is up next.

"Hi, I'm Camila. I'm experienced in front of the camera and have been a model in *SCENE* magazine. I'd love to meet you and hear how I can become an actor in Hollywood."

Oh, yeah. I forgot Camila was featured last year in an ad eating an ice-cream cone from Ben and Jerry's on the square. Now, in her ChitChat video for Lexi, she announces different emotions and then peers into the camera with that expression supposedly on her face. One is surprised. One, angry. One, madly in love. Honestly, I can't really tell the difference.

While more of my classmates pop up on the screen, I set my computer up and check the angles on the camera. It's as good as it's going to get. Deep breath. My hands tremble. I hit record.

"Hi," I say quickly. "I'm Maisie."

Almost immediately, I hold up a card that covers my face.

You are my hero, Lexi. I flip the card.

My dream is to be a graphic artist. I flip to the next card.

Just like you. I flip to the final card.

Will you check out my drawings?

Then I hold up the final card, which shows a strip from *The Froot Loops*—the scene where Grace morphs into a golden Lab in the bathroom to comfort the girl.

And just like that it's over. All my anxiety and worry and planning and preparation. Done. Off the video goes.

Showing that drawing to the world on ChitChat—even if the video will eventually disappear—took every ounce of courage I could muster. Now there's nothing to do but wait and see what Lexi thinks.

To take my mind off the whole thing, I log in to Sienna's account and send a message to Dezirea.

SIENNA: WHAT IS IT WITH YOU AND YOUR AWESOMENESS? YOUR VIDEO WAS AMAZEBALLS!!!! HONESTLY CANNOT HANDLE THE TALENT!

DEZIREA: THANKS. YOU REALLY THOUGHT SO?

SIENNA: YES!!!

DEZIREA: MOOD ☹

SIENNA: WHY?? YOU WERE FANTASTIC!

DEZIREA: I WISH I COULD DANCE MORE. I'D LOVE TO BE A BALLERINA. BUT IT'S NEVER GOING TO HAPPEN.

SIENNA: DON'T SAY NEVER

DEZIREA: TOO LATE NOW. HAVEN'T TAKEN LESSONS IN A WHILE. DAD THOUGHT IT WASN'T A GOOD INVESTMENT. NOW I'M TOO OLD AT 16.

SIENNA: MISTY COPELAND DIDN'T START BALLET UNTIL SHE WAS 13.

DEZIREA: HOW DID YOU KNOW THAT? *IMPRESSED*

SIENNA: I'M A HUGE FAN.

SIENNA: MAYBE YOUR MOM CAN CONVINCE YOUR DAD ABOUT THE LESSONS.

I cringe, realizing I may have slipped up. Sienna wouldn't know Dezirea's mom always talks her dad into spoiling her, but I do. When she turned seven, Dezirea wanted a carnival-themed birthday party. Her mom was the one who finally convinced her father to rent tents, face painters, and even a pony.

DEZIREA: MY MOM LIVES FIVE HOURS AWAY.

When did this happen?

SIENNA: YOUR PARENTS ARE DIVORCED?

DEZIREA: YES. LAST YEAR.

I'm not sure what to say. The pause must make her realize I'm uncomfortable.

DEZIREA: IT'S OKAY. THEY'RE HAPPIER APART.
BELIEVE ME.

But are you happier? I want to ask.

DEZIREA: WHAT ABOUT YOUR PARENTS?

SIENNA: THEY ARE STILL TOGETHER.

I can't imagine them not. They argue, but there is never any doubt they love each other.

DEZIREA: ANY SIBLINGS?

SIENNA: I HAVE A SISTER. SHE WENT TO COLLEGE THIS
YEAR.

DEZIREA: YOU MISS HER?

So, so much.

SIENNA: YES, I DO.

It's the first time I've actually told anyone. Only it's not really me sharing my feelings. Or is it? Where does Sienna stop and I start?

DEZIREA: MY LITTLE BROTHER IS IN MIDDLE SCHOOL. HE'S TAKING THE PARENT SPLIT PRETTY HARD, BUT HE TRIES TO PLAY THE WHOLE TOUGH GUY THING AND KEEPS IT ALL INSIDE.

I blink in surprise. I remember Dezirea's little brother as a skinny, annoying pest. Most of the time she was trying to get rid of him, but now she worries about him.

DEZIREA: I LIKE THAT I CAN TELL YOU THIS WITHOUT FEELING LIKE A COMPLETE IDIOT ABOUT IT.

SIENNA: IF YOU EVER NEED TO VENT, I'M YOUR GIRL. EVERYBODY NEEDS SOMEONE TO TALK TO.

Maybe this is wrong. Maybe I'm wrong.

DEZIREA: IT'D BE GREAT TO MEET YOU IRL.

SIENNA: YOU TOO.

DEZIREA: THEN LET'S DO IT!

SIENNA: WHAT? WHEN?

DEZIREA: TONIGHT! COME HANG OUT WITH ME AND MY CREW.

I can't believe what I'm reading. The most popular girl in the sophomore class just invited my imaginary shape-shifting self to hang out. My heart aches a little for what could have been. If I looked like Sienna, I could go. And maybe have a great time. I'll never know. I don't want to turn Dezirea down, though. Instead, I offer an alternative I'm sure she won't accept.

SIENNA: I CAN'T TONIGHT. I COULD COME TO TOWN TOMORROW AFTERNOON, BUT I NEED TO PICK UP A DRESS AT H&M AT THE MALL. WHY DON'T YOU MEET ME THERE?

Good. That makes Sienna seem busy and just a little bit elusive. Dezirea expects people to jump at her every request.

DEZIREA: SURE. WHAT TIME?

Oh. My. God. Power rush. I do a fist pump. Yes. This is a horribly dreadful game I'm playing, but I can't stop now. Because it's working. She's actually going to ditch her friends to come meet me . . . I mean Sienna? I feel like I have superpowers and it is amazing.

CHAPTER THIRTEEN

The next afternoon, I sit on a bench outside H&M waiting to see if Dezirea actually shows up. Maybe she's as big a fake as I am. A round old man with an equally elderly corgi stroll past slowly. The corgi stops to sniff at my foot and I reach down to pet his head. They both eventually totter off toward Macy's and I look up to see Dezirea walking right toward me.

I stare at her like an idiot, mouth open. No way.

Way.

She holds her phone in her hand and her head is bowed, eyes glued to the screen. I sink down into the bench, trying to make myself smaller and less conspicuous. The air tastes thick and I'm having a hard time breathing. But then I remember that even if she sees me, she won't know I'm Sienna. She walks past and into the store without once looking up from her phone. I am invisible. My shoulders relax into the new reality.

I just made Dezirea Davis come to the Foothills Mall. *How could this happen? How could I do this? Me?* The lowest person in the whole social strata of high school has somehow manipulated the most popular person on the planet to do exactly what I want. In this instant, I am no more. New skin. New face. New life. New friends.

The moment feels so right, so perfect. The sparkly wonder of it all is only slightly tainted with guilt. Everyone knows the best superheroes have a dark side.

I walk out to my car in the parking lot. When I get behind the wheel and close the door, I can't help but think what it would be like to meet Dezirea at the mall as me—as the friends we once were. Without lies or pretend faces. I stare out the window and think about how much better that would feel. It takes me a full minute and it makes my heart hurt a little. I exhale shakily, then start the car.

At home, I open the front door and walk inside, slipping off my sneakers and placing them beside my mom's shoes. The custom of removing our shoes when entering the house is one of my father's Filipino influences we all abide by. When I glance up, there is a girl about my age standing in the hallway. I blink. She looks familiar, but I don't know her.

Or do I?

She turns to face me and smiles, tucking her dark blonde hair behind one ear. Her dress is the color of lime sherbet—a pale, bright color I would never wear—and shows off her slim body to perfection.

Wait. No. It can't be.

My breath is coming short.

She wears strappy sandals that perfectly match the shade of her dress, her toenails bright pink and newly pedicured.

No. This can't be happening.

"Maisie," my mom says, coming into the hallway with a woman about her age, who has graying blonde hair. I barely see either of them. "You remember my colleague, Professor Zimmerman? Beth, you remember my daughter, Maisie?"

The woman beside Mom smiles. "You're so grown up! Last time I saw you, you were a little kid."

I can't answer.

"We're working on that Department of Education grant that needs to go out next week," Mom tells me.

I hear my mom speaking, but nothing is really sinking in. All I can do is stare at the girl in front of me.

"And this is her daughter, Claire," Mom goes on. "You guys are the same age, so I told Beth to bring Claire along today since they were driving up from Denver. I thought you two could hang out together while Beth and I work."

Beth beams at me. "Isn't that a terrific idea?" she asks.

It is a horrible idea.

Because Claire is THE Claire. The girl I found on ChitChat. The girl I thought I had no connection to. The girl I chose to be the face of Sienna.

She's here, in my house.

CHAPTER FOURTEEN

"So it's okay with you?" Claire asks me, looking utterly unimpressed.

Sienna is here. In the flesh. *Real*. I glance around, as if someone from school might somehow see her. As if I need to hide her away.

"Why don't you take Claire up to your room?" My mom waves us toward the stairs, making me feel like I'm about six years old and having a playdate. Claire's mother, Beth, is already spreading papers across our dining room and pulling out a laptop from her briefcase.

I want to scream, but instead take a deep breath and try to gather my thoughts.

"Follow me," I tell Sienna—or rather, Claire.

I lead the way up the stairs, hearing Claire walking behind me, but not wanting to look back over my shoulder.

This isn't happening. Think. Think. Think.

When we walk into my room, Claire does a quick assessment, then immediately goes to my desk. She looks at the pictures on the wall, then down at the sketches spread out over the desk.

"So what is all this . . . stuff?" Her hands are on her perfectly normal-sized hips, and she leans in to look closer like she's peering at some animal in a zoo.

I take a deep gulp of air, my words fast and tight before I need to take another breath. "They're just some of my drawings."

She waits for me to say more, but I can't stop staring at her. She is taller than I thought she'd be from her photos. The top of my head only reaches her eye level. I can't help but notice the differences between her and me. I'm short; she's tall. I have dark hair; she is blonde. I am fat. She's . . . not.

She looks back at me over her shoulder, shocked. "You did these?"

I nod. The strange sensation of watching her mouth move and actual words coming out of her face is mesmerizing. She isn't supposed to be real.

"Seriously?"

She's so interested in the drawings, she has no idea I'm staring at her like she's suddenly morphed into a Teenage Mutant Ninja Turtle. I nod again.

"Wow. This is amazeballs," she exclaims. She picks up a few of my *Froot Loops* sketches from the desk, scrutinizing them carefully. "So you're like an artist?"

I notice Claire starts almost every sentence with the word *so*. Sienna would never do that. It's annoying. "Something like that," I say.

Claire carefully lays the pictures back on the desk, then points at my bulletin board full of Lexi Singh prints. "What's this?"

"Lexi Singh? She's a famous graphic artist. The television show *Nosy Parker* is based on her comics. Do you know it?"

"Of course I watch that show. Everyone does. It's lit." Her blue eyes get huge, staring back at me. "Do you know her?"

"No, but she went to my high school. She's coming back for homecoming next week. I'm going to try to meet her."

Claire fake hits me on the shoulder. "Get out!"

I like the fact that I'm impressing her, but she's so different from the cool, calm Sienna I created. She plops down on my bed, not waiting for an invitation. I sit at my desk across the room from her.

"So where do you go to school?" I watch Claire/Sienna's mouth move, but there is a delay in my comprehension. This must be what Dr. Frankenstein felt like when he saw his monster come to life. Only Claire looks nothing like a monster.

"I'm a sophomore at Fort Collins High School," I finally say. "You?"

"I go to Denver West High School, for now," she says, lying back on the bed and staring up at the ceiling. "But we might be moving here."

My heart stops. "Why?" I blurt out.

"My mom might get transferred." She shrugs. "Do you like it here?"

No. It's horrible. And you would hate it. I swallow hard to keep from blurting everything out in a panic. Instead I say, "It's a pretty small town compared to Denver. Not nearly as much to do."

She nods, sitting back up to look at me. "Yeah, that's what I thought. Mom keeps trying to convince me, but I'm totally against it."

Within seconds her phone is in her hand and she's scrolling, head down, like I'm not even here. I wait, feeling like I've been emptied out and filled with helium.

"What's your ChitChat account?" Claire asks me, her eyes still glued to her screen.

"I don't have one," I lie. It's an automatic response. I have to keep Claire as far away as I can from everyone who might recognize her as Sienna.

She glances up from her phone and rolls her eyes. *"Everyone* has one."

"Not me." I chew on my lower lip, thinking. This needs to be believable so she won't go searching for me online. I say, "I want to spend all my extra time on my art."

"That makes sense. You know . . . for you." She gives me an I-feel-sorry-for-you look, then buries her head back in her phone.

I stare at her, transfixed, and chew on a nail.

Suddenly, Claire snaps to, holding one hand over her mouth and waving the other wildly in my direction.

"Oh. My. God. So I have the most absolutely brilliant idea."

I'm nervous. "What?"

"Do you think you could draw me as one of your comic book characters? Like Nosy Parker." Claire claps her hands together like a two-year-old. "My friends would die."

She stretches out the word *die* into about ten syllables.

I blink, an idea slowly starting to form in my buzzy mind. A perfectly awful idea. I push it away, but it comes back stronger and more defined. My brain feels like it's on fire.

I open my mouth, but my throat closes up on the words. I swallow, then say, "I'd need to take some photos. You know, to refer back to when I'm drawing you."

She nods, her eyes wide. "Totally."

I look at the floor, acting like I'm thinking it over, but I know my mind is already made up. "Okay. I'll do it."

Claire squeals, rolls over, and buries her head in my Wonder Woman pillow. She flutter-kicks her feet excitedly against my comforter. When she finally pulls the pillow off her head, she says, "I can't believe I'm going to be superhuman!"

I know how you feel.

I can't believe you're human.

"This is so cool. I might even make it my profile pic."

"Cool," I echo, grabbing my phone. "Can I start taking pictures?"

"Sure." Claire giggles. "Like I've ever turned down a photo op."

Why should you?

Claire poses while I snap tons of pictures. I figure I'll filter out anything identifying in the background, but for now I just enjoy the feeling of breaking through my hopelessness. In one picture, Claire sits cross-legged on my black checked throw rug smiling up at the camera. In another, she reads at my desk, looking super studious. In still another, she looks pensively out the window at the fall leaves. That's my favorite so far, but the view gives me more ideas.

"It's a beautiful day," I say. "The perfect backdrop. How about we take some pics outside?"

Luckily, Owen and Grace, who live nearest to me, are not around today; Owen is helping Grace out at the Humanity house. So neither of them would have any reason to drive past. Plus, I know Jesse is at football practice. And Dezirea is probably still at the mall.

Claire nods.

I look at her, eyes squinting. "Can you take your hair down?"

Clair doesn't question my choice. She immediately pulls out a mirror from her bag and goes to work on restyling her hair.

"Maybe a little eyeliner?" I suggest, and she nods enthusiastically, pulling out a makeup bag from her Kate Spade straw purse. I feel like a creative director, watching her apply eye shadow and helping select the right shade of gloss.

On the way out the door, she asks, "Coat or no coat?"

"Definitely coat," I say. It's time to mix up the outfits for the pictures.

I take more photos outside. Claire leaning against a tree. Claire sitting on a picnic table. Then I film some short action videos of Claire laughing and throwing leaves toward the camera. I even give her some lines to say.

"This time say *Wish you were here*," I call out from behind my phone.

Claire doesn't even ask why. "Wish you were here," she calls out as she tosses the leaves above her head.

Later, we hang out in my bedroom eating peanut butter and jelly sandwiches. I've now gotten more used to Sienna's— Claire's—presence. It feels almost normal that she's here.

Almost.

"So there's a school dance next weekend," she says.

"Sounds like fun," I say, trying to seem interested. All I want to do is look at the photos and select the perfect ones for Sienna to post.

"The football players may not be there. It's just not cool enough for them."

"Okay," I say, because I'm not sure what she wants from me.

"So I'm thinking I won't go." Claire meets my gaze over a half-eaten peanut butter and jelly sandwich. She sits up on one elbow.

"Why?" I ask.

Claire looks disappointed and sighs heavily, as if just having a polite conversation with someone like me is a major triumph. Now that the camera is no longer focused on her, we don't have much in common. She shrugs. "What would be the point?"

To dance. To have fun. To listen to music.

Claire's phone buzzes and she reads a text. "Ashley wants me to send a picture of you. She doesn't believe I'm really going to be a comic book star."

"No," I say quickly. "I don't like pictures."

Claire eyes me, her brows furrowed. "Because . . . you know . . . you're *plus-sized*?" she asks.

"Yeah," I say dryly. "Because of that."

"So I read this article last week on *Bustle* and it was all about body positivity. You should read it."

"Uh-huh," I say, picking up my phone and scrolling through the photos I took earlier. Claire looks beautiful in every one, even when she's not posing. She is the perfect Sienna in every way.

"So there were pictures of this really fat . . . I mean *big* . . . girl doing all these yoga poses and she was great just the way she was." Claire smiles at me. "You just have to realize you are beautiful on the inside. Looks don't matter."

Pretty girls are allowed to say that. Maybe they even believe it.

I stop scrolling and look up from my phone. Trying my best not to lose it, I close my eyes and exhale. Unfortunately, when I open them I see Claire polishing off her last bite of sandwich and I go off. I can't control the tone of my voice.

"Looks matter, Claire," I say bitterly. "If someone posts a photo of me online, I immediately get random comments that I'm fat or ugly. Sometimes that I'm fat *and* ugly. Sometimes the comments are from complete strangers who just need to share their opinion with the world, and sometimes they are from the people I pass in the hallway at school every day."

Claire seems surprised at my response, but she manages to interrupt me. "So I get comments on my photos, too. Not everybody likes them."

"You still don't get it. I *know* I'm not supposed to care. I *know* I should shake it off. But they make memes of me." I put my hands down on the desk and lean into Claire's face. "How would you like to be someone's worst insult?"

Claire meets my outburst with confused silence. She honestly has no idea what I'm talking about. And she never will.

"It may not show up in pictures, but I'm not always the smartest person in the room," Claire says quietly. Then she looks away.

I blink. Then blink again. Her words sink in. Perfect Sienna—Claire—isn't so perfect.

"People can be mean to you because of things they can see and because of things they can't, but it feels bad either way."

I take a deep breath and put my phone down on the desk. "You're right, Claire. I'm sorry."

When Claire's mom calls up the stairs that it's time to leave, I walk Claire downstairs.

"Did Claire tell you we might be moving?" her mom asks.

Claire makes a face. "But probably not."

"She's not that crazy about the idea. Maybe if she visited your school she'd see it wasn't so bad?" Beth asks me.

My stomach falls.

"I think that's a great idea," my mom says.

No. Absolutely not. There is NO WAY that can happen.

Then it just gets worse. "We have a couple of days off next week for teacher conferences," Beth goes on. "Maybe we can come back to Fort Collins and you can show Claire around?" she asks me brightly.

I want to turn around and run away. Then I realize it's better I try to control the situation than just let Claire show up.

"Sure," I mumble. "Probably after school would be best," I add.

When no one is around.

"Great." Her mom beams at me. "We'll text you."

After Claire and her mom leave, I sit on my bed and stare out the window, still in shock from what happened today.

There is a storm brewing. The kind where the thunder rumbles across the sky almost continuously, though there is no sign of actual lightning yet. But I know it's there.

The clouds are visibly angry—rippled and darker around the edges. They march slowly across the sky: pale gray falling off into dark black ridges. Another loud crash of thunder is followed by more slow rumbles.

Wind pounds at the sides of the house and rattles the windows with a roar. It's not unusual this time of the year here in Fort Collins. We get these random windstorms that blow in off the Rocky Mountains, down the foothills, and tear into the town. The gusts usually foretell a major change in temperature, but their power always surprises me. It can rip at trees and scatter patio furniture like a toddler tearing down a tower of blocks in a playroom.

Today the wind mirrors my brain, racing wildly. And it's not just wind to me. It makes me feel restless. Worried. Like the world is blowing with a power I can't control. Did Claire really just come into my life? What if she *does* come back to Fort Collins? What if she *moves* here? I am in no way prepared for this. How could I have seen it coming?

A monster is raging outside and it is oh so close to breaking its way into my life. It will tear me apart in a roar of satisfaction and I'll scatter about just like the patio cushions and trash cans. Just the sound of it, banging and pounding against my windows, raises my anxiety.

It's too much to deal with. I pull down my shades, try to ignore the wind, and scroll through the photos I took of Claire. At least I can make the best out of the situation.

I pause on a photo of Claire laughing at some strip she just read on my wall. Her head is thrown back, her smile wide and contagious. *Which one looks most like Sienna?* The phone seeps cold into my hand. If guilt was a color, it would be a sludgy purple stain that spreads up my fingers.

I feel guilty. Just not guilty enough to stop.

I post a couple of the new photos we took this afternoon and one of the videos. Watching Claire throwing leaves up in the air on endless repeat, I suddenly feel a flood of paranoia. What if *Claire* somehow discovers Sienna online? *It would never happen . . . It's too long a shot*, I tell myself. *And yet, maybe not.* Quickly, I find Claire's profile and block her—first as Sienna and then as Maisie. This way she'll never be able to find me or Sienna on ChitChat.

Breathing a little easier, I create a couple of new fake friends—using pictures culled from the internet and other random ChitChat profiles—and link them to Sienna's account. I've been adding a few such new friends every time I log in, so by now Sienna has gained almost twenty imaginary friends. If I think about it too much I realize each of those friends need friends and so on and so on, but where will that end? It's an endless black hole of deception. I log in and out from my various fake accounts, liking and commenting on Sienna's posts, photos, and videos to make it look like she has tons of friends.

EVERY PIC OF YOU LOOKS FLAWLESS.

ABSOLUTELY GORGEOUS. YOU'RE A GODDESS.

I WISH MORE PEOPLE WERE LIKE YOU.

Every time I write a new comment, I roll my eyes. *Do people really have friends who write this kind of idiotic stuff? Does it work?*

Then a new ChitChat message pops up. It's from Dezirea, and I realize I've forgotten all about what happened at the mall.

DEZIREA: WHERE WERE YOU TODAY?

SIENNA: I WAS AT THE MALL, WHERE WERE YOU?

DEZIREA: DIDN'T SEE YOU!

SIENNA: YOU CAME? WHAT TIME? I MUST HAVE JUST MISSED YOU! I'M SOOOOOO SORRY! GOT TIED UP AT FOREVER 21 BUYING THIS HEATHERED LONGLINE COAT.

DEZIREA: DID YOU SEE MY CHITCHAT MESSAGES?

SIENNA: NO. PHONE HAS BEEN GLITCHY LATELY. BATTERY WAS TOTALLY DEAD.

DEZIREA: UGH. THAT'S ANNOYING.

Time to change the subject.

SIENNA: WE CAN STILL GET TO KNOW EACH OTHER BETTER. PICK A SUPERPOWER. INVISIBILITY OR FLIGHT?

DEZIREA: DANCE.

SIENNA: LOL. THAT WASN'T A CHOICE.

DEZIREA: IT FEELS LIKE FLYING TO ME SOMETIMES.

SIENNA: WHY?

DEZIREA: EVERYONE IS ABLE TO MOVE TO MUSIC, BUT NOT EVERYONE WILL ACTUALLY PUT THE TIME IN TO DO IT UNTIL THEY'RE REALLY GOOD AT IT. BUT WHEN YOU'RE REALLY GOOD AT IT, IT IS BETTER THAN FLYING.

SIENNA: WOW. YOU MUST BE AN AMAZING DANCER.

DEZIREA: NOT MANY BALLET DANCERS LOOK LIKE ME.

SIENNA: DOESN'T MEAN YOU CAN'T DO IT.

DEZIREA: JUST FEEL LIKE SOMETHING DIED WHEN I STOPPED BEING ABLE TO TAKE CLASSES. SORRY YOU DIDN'T ASK FOR THIS.

SIENNA: IT'S OK. WE ALL FEEL THAT WAY SOMETIMES. IF YOU EVER NEED TO RANT, I'M YOUR GIRL. DON'T HOLD IT ALL IN.

DEZIREA: HOW ABOUT YOU? WHAT DO YOU WANT?

What does Sienna want? I never thought about it before. In this crazy alternative universe I've created, Sienna is me. I am Sienna. So she wants what I want, right?

SIENNA: I WANT TO LOVE MYSELF IN MY OWN SKIN.

DEZIREA: DON'T WE ALL?

CHITCHAT DIRECT MESSAGE

JESSE: ME AGAIN. WEARING OUT MY WELCOME YET?

SIENNA: HEY U. GOOD DAY?

JESSE: PRETTY GOOD.

JESSE: I TALKED TO A GIRL AT SCHOOL ABOUT YOU. AND OH THE QUESTIONS THAT CAME RAINING DOWN!

SIENNA: WHAT DID YOU SAY? TELL MEEEEEEE!

JESSE: I MOSTLY MADE UP A BUNCH OF STUFF ☺ ALL GLAMOROUS, OF COURSE!

SIENNA: OF COURSE!

JESSE: SHE'S DYING TO VISIT YOUR CHALET IN THE ALPS.

SIENNA: SRSLY??

JESSE: TOLD HER I THINK ABOUT YOU AND REALLY LIKE TALKING TO YOU.

JESSE: MORE THAN LIKE.

JESSE: YOUR MESSAGES ARE THE FIRST THINGS I LOOK FOR WHEN I OPEN CHITCHAT.

SIENNA: IF I WERE WITH YOU RIGHT NOW, I'D BE GIVING YOU A HUG YOU COULDN'T ESCAPE FROM.

JESSE: WOW. I LIKE THE WAY THAT SOUNDS.

CHAPTER FIFTEEN

On Sunday afternoon, Jesse is already at the library table by the window with books and papers spread out in front of him.

"You're late," he says.

"Sorry." I don't give any excuses. Outside the window, the first snow of the year is covering cars and tables. The same tables where a few days ago people sat in shorts and sandals, with dark glasses at the ready for the bright high-altitude sunshine. Yawning, I pull out my chemistry notebook from my bag.

He gives a sideways grin and says, "You wild woman. Partying until dawn every night is going to catch up to you."

Talking on the computer to you every night is going to catch up to me.

He looks good as always, with his dark, spiky hair and thick eyebrows. The sleeves of his faded blue Nike T-shirt stretch tightly across his biceps as he reaches for the lab write-up directions. It feels surreal to sit here across from him as though nothing has happened between us.

But nothing has. Not really.

I remember the day I first laid eyes on Jesse Santos. He looked different then. I guess we both did. At twelve, I was already getting smaller inside and bigger on the outside. I wasn't so sharply drawn anymore. I spoke up less and not so loudly. I was already slipping away off the page. My image had started to blur around the edges.

It was a perfect day for hanging out at the pool, but I remember being self-conscious for the first time. I slumped into the lounge chair, hoping the plastic would hold my weight and that I could eventually pull myself out without drawing any attention.

Dezirea lazed on the chair beside me in a hot pink bikini, soaking up the sun like a lazy cat finding a patch of light on the carpet. I pushed my sunglasses up the bridge of my nose and pulled my floppy sun hat down a little lower on my face. Last year's bathing suit was way too small, and I didn't like the way the shiny blue one-piece stretched over my new curves.

I wore a loose T-shirt over the swimsuit, and I couldn't imagine pulling it off in front of the crowd even though the cool blue water looked so enticing. There were at least fifteen kids there when my dad let me out and waved good-bye and there were more now. One of the boys from our school, Michael Garcia, was chasing two screaming girls along the side of the pool until the lifeguard whistle stopped him in his tracks. Two other kids were yelling

"Marco Polo" in the deeper water, and a girl I recognized from choir was splashing around in the shallow water with a couple of smaller kids.

Before this summer, swimming pools were refreshing escapes, where I could float away with all my thoughts. But now everyone looked older. Everywhere I looked I saw two-piece bathing suits and no T-shirts.

The longer we lay there, the hotter and sweatier I felt. In the middle of the pool, one big boy tumbled backward into the water and off the shoulders of some other blond brick of a boy. Then there was a lot of splashing and laughing. Everything about it looked fun. I wanted it so bad. And it was so close.

We were at City Park Pool to celebrate the first days of summer. In only a few months, the dynamics of our world would change forever.

We would go to middle school. Dezirea was growing up. I didn't want to yet.

Soon all the kids from three different elementary schools would converge into one middle school. New friends would be made, and old ones would be lost. It was inevitable. We just didn't realize it at the time.

"Hey. My name is Jesse." The boy standing beside our chairs was brown-skinned and dark-haired. He had braces on his teeth and the confidence to not care about wearing a shirt to cover up his pudgy tummy. He'd stopped in front of us and for a minute I thought he might actually sit down right on the end of my lounge chair. My throat felt suddenly pinched. Now I really didn't want to take my shirt off.

Dezirea looked up at him and raised one eyebrow, assessing the newcomer. "I'm Dezirea and this is Maisie," she finally said, but her eyes focused past him and on the group of boys playing chicken in the pool.

"So guess what I just learned," Jesse said, settling on to the ground beside me. There was a thin film of sweat across his forehead. "They just invented a special dye to put in the water that turns it green anytime someone pees."

I rolled my eyes. "That's an urban legend. It's the most common pool myth of all time."

"No, I swear." Jesse peered out at me from underneath a thick lock of dark hair. "Besides, a lot of technological advances have happened recently. It could be true now. Do you want to take the risk?"

Does he think I'm going to pee in the pool?

"Shut up," I said, but I was smiling.

"How about it? Are you going in?" Jesse nodded toward the pool.

Say yes.

He stood up and extended his hand. I thought about taking off my cover-up. It was a long walk to the steps on the other side of the pool—one that led right past a giggling gaggle of older girls watching the group roughhousing in the water. Those girls never intended to get their perfect bathing suits wet, even though they were at a swimming pool. Instead, they squealed and dodged every time one of the boys came close to getting them wet. It was a gauntlet I wasn't willing to brave.

"Maybe later," I said, hating the way I cared.

"I'll go," Dezirea said. She stood and stalked off toward the pool in one fluid motion, not even glancing back once.

Jesse paused a beat, looked at me as though he was almost disappointed, then said, "Okay."

They walked, side by side, around the edge of the pool. Dezirea moved with a dancer's grace, her back straight and her chin held high. Nothing bounced. Nothing wiggled. Nothing squeezed out around the edges of that bikini. Jesse trailed along behind, clumsy and too big for his skin.

An eighth-grade popular girl stopped chatting with all her friends to pull her Gucci knockoff sunglasses down her nose and peer at the two of them. I glanced at Dezirea's empty chair, then back toward the pool.

The squeals from the game of chicken drowned out most of the other noise around the pool, but Dezirea was oblivious. And fearless. She headed for the deep end and did a yelling, splashy cannonball that drenched the front row of the watching girls. I smiled at the reaction of shocked admiration from the crowd. Jesse stood frozen on the edge of the pool, his mouth dropped open in amazement.

I sat there alone huddled under my cover-up and wished it could be me. *So. Hard.*

The anger built slowly and deeply over the years. Nothing about our world seemed the same for girls like me. I was left out and treated differently than the other, more normal-sized girls. And I couldn't change the world. I couldn't even change me.

There is no sign of that boy at the pool sitting across from me now. Today, he is football star Jesse Santos. All those chubby rolls on Middle School Jesse morphed into a solid rectangular block of a guy that coaches dream about. The braces came off his teeth, he grew six inches, and he gave up playing the trumpet for protecting the quarterback from oncoming linemen.

I notice Jesse watching a cute girl across the library. A hand-knitted green beanie just barely covers her thick shoulder-length bob. Wearing a short plaid miniskirt and bright yellow tights, she looks like she just walked off the page of one of Lexi's comic books. She takes a copy of *The Lord of the Rings* over to a red couch in the corner. She crosses one long leg over the other and leans back against the cushions, opening the book. Jesse suddenly looks over and catches me watching her, but he just smirks.

"Can you just *concentrate*?" I snap at Jesse.

"You're one to talk. I'm ready to go and you haven't even looked at your notes yet."

Jesse gives me the handout and we start to read the material silently. Then he interrupts the peace and quiet to start reading aloud.

"Attractions happen between opposite charges. Repulsions happen between like charges." He looks up at me. "So it's like everyone says, opposites attract."

I snort a laugh. "Yeah, right. Life is not exactly chemistry class. People like people exactly like them."

"Do you honestly believe that?" he asks me.

I nod.

"Okay." He looks back down at the sheet in his hands. "It says here we have to support our claims using valid reasoning and sufficient evidence. So prove it."

"I have verified the results so many times and so many ways, you could call it a scientific fact," I say flatly.

"Support your claims," he insists. He grins and taps the end of my nose with his pen.

I pull away, rolling my eyes. "All right," I say. "Here's the procedure. Follow it closely."

Jesse nods and readies his pen over the paper like he's going to take notes.

"Me and . . ." I look back across the room. ". . . the girl over there with the green beanie sit beside each other in a room. A good-looking boy enters. He is told to interact with us for a period of time."

"Who tells him?"

"It doesn't matter." I shake my head. "That's just the direction he's given."

"By, like . . . a scientist?"

"Sure. Okay. A scientist tells the boy to go in the room and talk to the girls."

Jesse nods, then his eyes widen intently. "Is the scientist a woman or a man?"

Seriously? "It doesn't matter."

"It might."

"Fine. The scientist is a woman."

"I thought so." He grins at me like he just figured out the murderer in a game of Clue. "And then what happens?"

"The boy's gaze will linger on *her* face." I nod toward the girl in the beanie.

Jesse's eyes narrow and his pen hovers over the blank paper.

I continue, "He will sit next to the cute girl. He will only look at the cute girl. He will talk to her for longer. If the scientist says he has to talk to BOTH, then he will ask me shorter questions and not wait for the answer. Because he doesn't want to know the answer. At least not from me."

Jesse's hair falls onto his forehead, and he brushes it back impatiently with his forearm. "There should be a playlist for this experiment. I'd put 'You Don't Know Me' on it. Maybe the Ray Charles version?" He writes that on his notepad.

I've never heard that song, but I know I will probably look for it later tonight. "Do you want to hear this or not?" I ask him.

He nods. "Keep going."

"*Her* answers to the boy's questions will make him smile—even laugh," I say. "At the end of the experiment, the scientist will ask the boy which girl he wants to spend more time with now."

Jesse's eyes shift for just a second. He knows how this will end.

"He will choose her," I say, nodding to the girl in the corner. We both watch as she sits up and begins rummaging through her bag again, finally pulling out a tube of EOS sparkle lip balm. She swipes the gloss across her lips, then buries her head back in the book, oblivious to her starring role in my story. "He won't remember my name, but he'll ask for her number."

Under his breath, Jesse says, "That's a sad experiment."

"If there is one thing I like about chemistry, it's that reactions are predictable," I say. "Every time."

Jesse looks skeptical. "I don't think you like this experiment of yours all that much."

I sigh. "It's the way the world is made."

Jesse watches me, his face unreadable.

I shrug and try to make a joke of it all. "Hydrogen doesn't look at oxygen and think, *Yeah, you're just not that attractive to me. I think I'll go combine with someone else and make some water. But I'm sure you have a great personality. You know. On the inside.*"

Jesse doesn't laugh, but he leans over and taps a finger on my forehead. I jerk away from his touch. "What is it like in that brain of yours? I'm thinking it's really, really crowded in there." He pauses, then adds, "In a cool way."

I look down at the table, flipping the pages of my notebook, but I can feel him smiling at me. My control is slipping away. This Jesse is too much like the Jesse I've been talking to on ChitChat.

He taps his pencil on my drawing of the fairy. "Did anyone ever tell you you're insanely talented?"

I shrug, feeling a deep flush move from my chest up my neck. "Most people have lots of friends. I have lots of drawings."

"You should share them online so others can see them."

"Maybe," I say, surprised at the suggestion. "I might not be able to cope with the huge onslaught of rabid fans."

Jesse grins. "Do it for the people who want to see you fail."

I turn the page to my chemistry notes, covering the drawing from prying eyes. "I don't like showing people this stuff."

"Well, guess what? You just showed me," he says, like that settles things.

I scowl at him. "It was an accident. You weren't supposed to see it."

"You showed a sketch for your Lexi Singh audition." He reaches out and flips back to my initial sketch of the fairy. "But this one looks different. The style is . . . bold. Raw. I like it."

Jesse watched my ChitChat application?

"My sister's an artist," Jesse is saying. "Not like that. She used to paint landscapes. Watercolor, mostly," he says.

"She was really good, and I hope she goes back to it one day."

"Why did she stop?"

"After the baby . . ." Jesse sets his jaw and stares straight ahead. He looks uncomfortable and he's not smiling. "I guess she just didn't have the heart for it."

"You're an uncle?"

"I was. He was three months too early." There is no cocky self-assuredness in his tone. It is unsettling and makes me uncomfortable. I don't know what to do with this Jesse Santos.

I'm afraid to ask, but I do. "Was?"

"He was a fighter, but he didn't make it." His jaw twitches. Then he blinks and looks back at me. "His name was Jesse, too. After me."

I don't know what to say. "I'm sorry."

"Yeah. Me too." He gives me a sad smile. "Okay. Enough talking. We need to get this done because I have a thing I have to be at in an hour." He says it like he has an appointment to rush into a burning building to save a puppy.

"What thing?" I ask, but of course I know. He's going to the hospital to volunteer. I *cannot* let on that I know that, though. I can't let any piece of Sienna slip through.

But was he even telling Sienna the truth? It still seems like a stretch that Jesse would lie about something like that. But then how well do I actually know him?

He makes his face all scrunchy and says, "A *secret* thing." It's like a joke, but I know it's not.

"Where are you going for this *secret* thing?" I mimic his tone and exaggerate the word *secret*.

"Oh, no. I'm not giving you any info. You'd be just the type to stalk me." He laughs like that's funny, but my stomach tightens. It's all too close to the truth.

I nod, and we get back to work.

☞   ☞   ☞

When Jesse leaves the library, I follow him in my car. He takes a right turn onto Timberline, then a left at the light. I don't get too close. There's not much traffic, so it's easy to follow from a distance. When he turns into the Poudre Valley Hospital parking lot, I pull into a nearby lot and watch him go in the main entrance. He doesn't look up from his phone.

The hospital elevator is huge, with two doors on either side. I press the button for the fourth floor and stand toward the middle because I don't know which side will open. The hallway is wide, with colored stripes down the white tile directing visitors to various areas. Yellow for pediatrics. Blue for post op. Green for neonatal. I follow the green line down the hall, then take a sharp right. The wall in front of me is full of windows. An older couple stand outside looking in. They hold hands and lean forward, noses almost touching the glass.

Inside, I see Jesse and pull back to the edge of the window. He doesn't look my way, and I let out a breath of relief. He sits in a rocking chair over by an incubator. In his arms is a tiny bundle. His head rests against the tall wooden back of the rocking chair, and his eyes are closed. Nurses and doctors walk around the room, pausing at various stations and working. Jesse keeps rocking, eyes still closed.

So he wasn't lying.

I blink. Then blink again. My Grinch of a heart suddenly feels cramped in my chest.

Then the chair stops rocking and Jesse opens his eyes, looking down at the bundle in his arms. He smiles a wide grin down at the tiny face. His lips move and I know he is telling the baby something, even though I can't hear the words. Then he pulls the blanket a little tighter, carefully avoiding the tubes and monitors trailing from his lap, and leans back to close his eyes again, rocker reengaged.

Jesse Santos is real—with divorced parents and an older sister who lost her child. He likes jazz music and the color blue and purple Peeps and talking to a girl named Sienna. He rocks babies on Sundays.

I don't want to know these things. I need him to deserve my deceit. It's the only thing that makes my shape-shifting meaningful. Suddenly and fiercely, I want out of here. Everything feels sterile, strange, and confusing. I stumble off in the direction of the elevator, vaguely aware of the green line on the floor. When the silver doors slide open, I rush inside, punching at the ground floor button. My hands are shaking. I shove them deep in my pockets and step back until I feel the cold of the wall behind me.

I can't like him.

CHAPTER SIXTEEN

"I decided to ask Grace to the homecoming dance," Owen tells me proudly when we get in the car to go home from school on Monday. "It's this Friday."

"Yes, I know." *Everybody knows.*

But he evidently knew nothing about Grace's plan for the three of us to go together. Suddenly I feel excluded and grumpy. *Two's company, three's a crowd.*

He unzips the outside pocket on his book bag and slides out a cream-colored envelope. "I made her an invitation."

I nod and he slides the envelope carefully back into the pocket like it's a priceless treasure. He gives me a solemn nod. "I'm going to give it to her today."

I never had to share Owen with anyone before. I don't know how to do it. But most of all I don't *want* to do it. Snakes of jealousy slither into the darkest corners of my brain. I think they must be lime green with razor-sharp fangs of bitterness. My fingers itch for a pencil in my hand. I would draw them twisting and curling around my skull, hissing their poison deep into my eardrums.

Ssss-see? Sssss-seeee?

Big splashes of rain spatter across the windshield. It's

not cold enough for the drops to turn to snow today, but it's just cold enough to make things wet and miserable. I stop the car at our bench. Grace runs up to the car, books held over her head as a shield. She doesn't ask for a ride anymore. It's just expected.

She slides into the back seat and slams the car door, laughing. "Do you know why you have to be careful when it rains cats and dogs?"

"Because you might step in a poodle," I say in a monotone.

Graces makes a snorting sound with her nose, but it's not quite a laugh. She pulls a baggie out of her coat pocket. "Cheese crisps?"

"What are you so cheery about?" Owen asks, as if she isn't always this way. He takes a handful of the orange balls and hands a couple to me. I pop two in my mouth, chewing. Of course they are delicious, but who makes homemade cheese crisps?

Grace's head bobs up and down in the back seat, in and out of view of the rearview mirror. "I'm so excited for this weekend. We didn't have homecoming at my old school. It's all so thrilling!"

"The only exciting thing is that people might get to meet with Lexi," I say, clutching the steering wheel.

"I just know one of them is going to be you, Maisie," Owen says. Grace's positive look on the world has seeped into his brain.

"You're excited, too, right?" Grace asks me.

I mumble a response that could be yes or no while driving ahead.

"You okay?" Grace reaches over the seat to massage my shoulders.

I shrug her off. "I'm fine."

"I was thinking we should all go to the homecoming dance together," Grace announces. "We could dress up like the Justice League or something like that."

"We'd need two more people," I say dismissively.

"So we could be *part* of the Justice League," Grace says. "If you don't go, you know you'll regret it. It's time for us Froot Loops to take a stand and be ourselves!" She flips her hair over one shoulder and raises an arm up in the air.

She did NOT just call herself a Froot Loop! I feel my whole body go stiff. Even though Grace knows what it's like to be bullied, she doesn't know what Owen and I went through together.

"I don't think that's a good idea," I say. "Right, Owen?"

Owen shoots me a look like we are co-conspirators in something.

"It's just . . ." Owen's fingers fiddle restlessly with the door handle. "I might have other plans."

There's a stunned silence in the car. I glance in the rearview mirror and see Grace's disappointed face. I feel sorry for her despite myself.

Her eyes are welling up, and she wipes her right one on her coat sleeve. She looks at the back of Owen's head and the jealousy scuttles under my skin again, slinking deeper. I recognize it, but I cannot stop it. That's when I realize Grace likes Owen. And I know Owen likes Grace. *So where does that leave me?*

Grace tries desperately to recapture the mood with a silly joke. "You're acting like a nucleus surrounded by a cloud of negatively charged ions. Nobody needs that kind of energy."

"I think I'm moving on from humor," Owen says from the passenger seat. "It's time."

"To?" I'm almost afraid to ask.

"I haven't decided yet."

The light turns red. I close my eyes and lean my head back against the car seat. My thoughts are spinning. In a few days, I will find out if I get to meet with Lexi. I don't even want to imagine how it's going to feel if I don't make it. Everyone is walking toward a cliff and they will disappear forever when we all get to the edge. Owen will step blithely off into Grace's world, and I will be standing on top all alone.

"The light is green," Grace says in her most helpful voice.

What am I? The chauffeur?

When we pull up to Grace's house, she hops out and slams the door behind her, yelling good-bye over her shoulder.

Owen rolls down the window. "Grace?" She turns back to the car. "I want to ask you something."

Oh, no. Not here. Not now.

She leans in the open car window and Owen hands her the cream envelope with her name printed on the front. She looks down at it, then asks, "Is it a joke?"

"No." Owen blushes.

"Should I open it now?"

He glances over at me and I recognize his panicked look. "Sure," I say, putting the car in park and turning off the engine. "Go ahead and open it."

I make a motion with my head to encourage Owen to get out of the car. He stares back at me, confused, so finally I just say, "Get out and walk her to the door."

He nods nervously and jumps out, slamming the door behind him.

At first, I stare straight ahead and wait. A squirrel scampers across in front of the car and then up a tree on the other side. The mail truck pulls up to the boxes at the end of the street. A jogger runs past on the sidewalk. I close my eyes tightly and count to ten. Owen still isn't back to the car. I close my eyes again and count to twenty.

Then I open my eyes and glance sideways. I can't help it. My heart twitches. Owen is standing so close to Grace their heads are almost touching. I blink hard. Grace wraps Owen in a massive hug and I can see his face over her shoulder. It hurts my heart. Yet I can see how much he wants this, and if I were truly his friend, I would want it for him, too. I wouldn't be selfish and petty. I'd want him to be happy. And I do. Deep down somewhere in this jealousy-filled heart, I honestly do.

CHITCHAT DIRECT MESSAGE

JESSE: CAN WE TALK?

SIENNA: WE ARE TALKING.

JESSE: U KNOW WHAT I MEAN. I WANT TO HEAR YOUR VOICE.

JESSE: FOR REAL. ON THE PHONE.

JESSE: ???

SIENNA: . . .

SIENNA: I CAN'T RIGHT NOW. MY PARENTS ARE HERE.

JESSE: WHERE R U?

SIENNA: AT DINNER. MAYBE LATER?

JESSE: PROMISE?

SIENNA: NO PROMISES.

JESSE: SO WHEN CAN WE MEET UP?

SIENNA: IT MAKES ME NERVOUS. WHAT IF YOU DON'T LIKE ME IN PERSON?

JESSE: I ALREADY LIKE YOU.

SIENNA: YOU KNOW WHAT I MEAN.

JESSE: THERE'S NOTHING TO WORRY ABOUT.

SIENNA: NOT WORRIED. JUST SHY I GUESS.

JESSE: AT LEAST THINK ABOUT IT?

JESSE: ARE YOU THINKING ABOUT IT?

JESSE: HOW ABOUT NOW?

JESSE: NOW?

SIENNA: STOP IT! 😊

JESSE: DID YOU LISTEN TO THE SONG I SENT YOU LAST NIGHT? "IN THE WEE SMALL HOURS OF THE MORNING"?

SIENNA: IT SEEMED APPROPRIATE SINCE YOU SENT IT AT 2 A.M.

JESSE: I COULDN'T SLEEP. IT'S A REALLY OLD FRANK SINATRA SONG, BUT THE JOHN MAYER VERSION WITH CHRIS BOTTI'S HORN IS MY FAVORITE.

SIENNA: I CAN SEE WHY. IT'S BEAUTIFUL.

JESSE: SO YOU DID LISTEN TO IT!

SIENNA: *CONFESSES* MAYBE A COUPLE OF TIMES.

JESSE: I COULD PLAY IT FOR YOU IN REAL LIFE.

SIENNA: I'LL THINK ABOUT IT.

CHAPTER SEVENTEEN

I usually dream in color, but tonight, the world is black and white. It is the white I see first—huge flakes of snow dancing down slowly from a black sky. The snow-covered path in front of the white horses is lined with dark trees, decorated in what looks like white spun-sugar icing. I'm sitting in the sleigh, snuggled into a thick fleece blanket and there is music—a single saxophone playing like a soundtrack behind the crunch of the hooves and the jingle of the harness bells.

"Are you cold?"

I jump at the sudden question. Jesse is here with me, black stocking cap pulled low over his dark eyes. I suddenly think those eyes are the most beautiful part of this magical scene.

I shake my head. "No," I say, and it's strangely true.

Jesse smiles, blinking one flake of snow from his long black lashes. He reaches out to cup my cheek in his hand. His eyes search my face like it's some kind of wonderful surprise.

He whispers, "You are amazing."

I laugh and touch his lips gently with one finger. "I am, aren't I?"

"We should go. They're waiting on us," Jesse says, flicking the reins and setting the horses off at trot through the forest.

Then we are inside, in a beachfront restaurant, in the summer. The colors burst into my brain like someone flipped on a box of crayolas. Long white curtains flap at the windows, open to a roaring sea view. Outside an orange sun dips halfway into the water, as the sunset turns the sky bright pink. Vases full of roses line the tables and fill the counters—bright pink shrub roses and deep red tea roses, rich yellow-gold ones and orange blooms with bloodred tips.

The restaurant hostess is Lexi Singh. "Can I show you to your table?" she asks.

"Your roses are so beautiful," I say.

She nods. "It's because they are real."

We follow Lexi through the café and out the door toward the beach. Heads swivel as we walk by and it feels wonderful. I recognize everyone here. Owen is the crow sitting at the corner table across from the Labrador.

I catch a reflection of myself in the window on the way out. I'm in my own shape and loving it. My shoulders are round and smooth in a bright green sundress. My legs are curved and bare.

I'm real, too.

Lexi sits us at a table right out on the sand and suddenly we are all alone.

Jesse leans across the space between us. "If you don't tell me to stop, I'm going to kiss you."

I reach up and pull his face down to mine, never so confident of anything in my life. My lips touch his, lightly. Just a brush. He draws back and sucks in a breath. Then I kiss him again and he kisses me back. The table disappears. There is no more beach. There is only us—kissing and kissing. His arms circle my waist, pulling me closer, and I don't flinch away.

Suddenly, I can't breathe. I pull back, feeling a tingle in my fingers. I hold my hands up in front of my face, watching in horror as my fingers start to dissolve from the tip of my nails down to my knuckles.

Jesse looks at me in horror. "What's happening?"

My hands are gone now and my arms are shattering into invisibility. I can't speak anymore. All I can do is watch myself disappear. The world swirls away into a snow globe of nothing.

I wake with tears on my cheeks. I'm not sure if I'm crying for the loss of Jesse . . . or for the loss of me.

"Have you ever talked to someone online you didn't know in real life?" Jesse asks me in class on Tuesday morning.

My breath catches in my throat. "Sure. I guess so."

"Did you ever meet them?"

"I don't think so." My throat clenches so tight I can barely get the words out. Lingering memories from last night's dream flicker in and out of my brain, making it hard to look him in the eyes.

"There's this girl I've been talking to online. Sienna." He glances away. "But it's weird. She always has some kind of excuse for why she can't talk to me on the phone or meet me in person."

I open my mouth. Close it again. Then open it again. Nothing comes out.

"I'm beginning to think there's something not right about her."

"What do you mean?" My face burns and I can feel my fingers gripping the edge of the table in front of us.

"Maybe she's not . . . real."

"But you're talking to *someone*." My mind is speeding, careening around corners and squealing through stop signs.

"Yeah . . . but who?" He shrugs. "Maybe she's not who she says she is."

"Why would you think that?" A rock falls out of the wall of lies I built. It is all starting to crumble. I can't stop it.

Breathe in. Breathe out.

"She never video chats with me or even talks on the phone. That's always like a big red flag on all those cat-fishing shows."

"Maybe she's just busy. Not everyone's world revolves around you." I make my face smile so he knows I'm teasing him, but he doesn't seem to notice.

He's quiet. Then he says, "I know it sounds crazy, but you see those kinds of things happen on TV all the time, right?"

"I guess . . ." I make my voice sound doubtful. "But why would someone do that to you?"

He shakes his head. "I don't know. It doesn't make any sense."

I see a glimmer of light. There might be an end to this online charade. Once Jesse asks Sienna out and she says no, it will be over. My plan for revenge on Jesse Santos will be complete. He fell for an invisible girl who was really me—the object of his bullying.

"Maybe you should force the issue," I tell him.

"How?"

Push him.

"Ask her out. If she's faking it, there's no way she'll say yes."

"And if she does say yes?" he asks.

She won't. Trust me.

▷   ▷   ▷

In history class, the loudspeaker clicks on and Principal Buckton comes on to make a special announcement.

"Attention. Attention." There is a pause and everyone looks up to the speaker on the wall. From it, there comes the sound of someone awkwardly drumming their hands on the desktop. "I have in front of me a list of the winners of this year's homecoming court."

An excited chatter spreads through the class. I see Camila reach for Dezirea's hand, clutching it tightly.

The whole student body chooses the homecoming queen and king from the seniors. Juniors, sophomores, and freshmen also get to select a princess and prince for the court from their own respectives classes. Since it's a popularity contest, it's never really a surprise who is elected. But there is usually some drama about who the court members bring as their dates. Being the date of a member of royalty is the next best thing to being on the court.

"Congratulations to our homecoming king, Josiah Brown, and homecoming queen, Divinity Gates."

The applause is polite, but not enthusiastic. No one is shocked. Josiah is the quarterback for the football team and Divinity is senior class president, so it just makes sense. Principal Buckton then announces the junior prince, Sean Grier, and junior princess, Kathryn Cho. Again, no surprise.

"Now, for the sophomores." The principal clears her throat and I feel the suspense rise. This is the one most of the people in this room care about. Hunter crosses his fingers on both hands and holds them up by his ears, squeezing his eyes shut.

"Sophomore prince is Jesse Santos, and sophomore princess is Dezirea Davis."

I'm quiet, but everyone else breaks into applause and cheers. I haven't heard who Jesse asked to homecoming, but whoever it is will be on cloud nine when they realize it includes a starring role on the homecoming float. Camila hugs Dezirea and they both squeal so loudly no one even hears the names of the freshman prince and princess. Not that it really matters. Several guys congratulate Graham with fervent pats on the back, since everyone knows he'll be Dezirea's date.

"What are you going to wear?" Camila asks Dezirea, and immediately several girls near them start excitedly contributing suggestions.

"Okay, people." Mrs. White is facing a losing battle. No one is interested in World War I anymore. Like they ever were. "I realize everyone is excited about all the homecoming festivities, but we still have ten minutes left in class."

Groans from the audience.

Surprisingly, she relents, holding up her open hands in surrender. "Okay. Okay. Just this once. Free time until the bell rings, but keep the noise down."

My phone buzzes in my bag. When I pull it out, I'm surprised to see a message from Claire. My stomach drops. Why is she writing to me? Did she stumble upon Sienna's profile on ChitChat? I click open the message, cringing.

CLAIRE: OMG. THE DUMBEST THING HAPPENED. MY MOM DECIDED I HAVE TO TAKE A TOUR OF YOUR HIGH SCHOOL. TOMORROW! ☹

I stare down at the screen, dazed. Then I reread the text.

No. No. Noooooo. This is almost worse than Claire finding out about Sienna. Worse than her coming to my house. Claire can't possibly show up at my *school*. It would ruin everything. *Everything.*

I think fast and write back.

> **ME: THAT WOULD BE A WASTE OF TIME. IT'S REALLY NOT YOUR SCENE.**

> **CLAIRE: I KNOW, BUT MY MOM'S JUST NOT GETTING IT! SHE'S BEING REALLY STRICT ABOUT IT. SHE CALLED THE SCHOOL AND THEY SAID THIS GIRL NAMED DIVINITY COULD SHOW ME AROUND.**

I'm horrified. Divinity, as the senior class president, does give all the tours. This is actually happening. My worlds are colliding.

> **ME: YOU'RE NOT GOING TO DO IT, ARE YOU?????**

> **CLAIRE: I DON'T WANT TO, BUT . . .**

I'm frozen in my seat.
But, what??? Think. Think. Think.

ME: MAYBE YOU COULD SAY YOU'RE SICK? TO GET OUT OF IT?

CLAIRE: MY MOM WON'T BUY THAT. ANYWAY, I MIGHT AS WELL GET IT OVER WITH.

I'm trembling. *I can't stop her. She's going to come here.* The horrifying reality sinks in. I need to be there to meet her, of course. I need to run interference and find a way to avoid having Claire bump into *anyone* that Sienna's talked to on ChitChat. Divinity is safe—she exists in a totally different ChitChat world. She doesn't know Sienna. But is there a way to have it *only* be Divinity that Claire sees?

There's one last desperate thing I can do.

ME: YOU KNOW IT HAS TO BE AFTER SCHOOL, RIGHT?

CLAIRE: WHY?

ME: TOURS FOR NEW STUDENTS ARE ONLY AFTER SCHOOL SO IT DOESN'T INTERRUPT CLASSES.

It's a total lie, of course. I hold my breath, hoping she won't question me, even though it doesn't make any sense.

CLAIRE: OK. 4 O'CLOCK?

That's not late enough.

ME: MAKE IT 4:30.

The hallways will be emptied out by then. If she has to show up, that's the best possible time. And I'll just ask Divinity to meet Claire then; she's always hanging around after school doing work in the student government office, so it won't be a big deal for her.

CLAIRE: OK. SHOULD I MEET YOU OUT FRONT?

That's way too public. The bell rings then and I type back quickly.

ME: I'LL TEXT YOU LATER ABOUT WHERE TO MEET.

CLAIRE: OK. IT WILL BE GREAT TO SEE A FAMILIAR FACE! ☺

I just hope no one recognizes YOUR face, I think. I stand up, my stomach clenching. I have no idea how I'm going to pull this off, but I have to try.

▷   ▷   ▷

The next day, at 4:30 p.m., I meet Claire at the side door that leads into an empty hallway. She followed my secret-agent-like directions perfectly to the most obscure entrance in the whole building. When I see her standing there, my heart does a little dive right into the pit of my stomach. I smile shakily at her and give a weak wave. I didn't sleep at all last night.

"Hey," I say, opening the door for us and glancing around warily. No one is here. At least, for now.

"Maisie," Claire squeals, grabbing me in a hug with one arm and holding her Venti Starbucks Frappuccino in her free hand. Her thick blonde hair is in a ballerina bun wrapped in winter white fabric that exactly matches her wool swing coat.

As we walk down the empty hallway, Claire does a little shrug to get out of her coat. Underneath, she wears a thick cable-knit sweater in the same shade of white. Her legs look long and lean, her skinny jeans tucked into brown leather riding boots. I feel strangely proud. This is exactly how Sienna would dress.

"So you really didn't have to do this," Claire tells me when we reach my locker.

Believe me, I didn't want to.

"No problem." I take her coat, fold it carefully, and store it in my locker. Then I take another quick look around to see if the coast is clear. *So far, so good.* This really is the best possible day—and time of day—Claire could have come. The football team is practicing for the big game, so there's no way Claire will run into Jesse. And everyone else is out decorating floats and buying costumes for the cosplay-themed dance. But I still need to be on high alert.

"So I still can't believe I'm going to be a comic book character!" Claire is saying. "That is so cool. I might even make it my profile pic. Can you show me what you've done so far?"

I frown. I forgot all about Claire's picture. "I'm—um, I'm sorry." I scramble for a response. "I can't really show you anything until I'm absolutely sure it's ready. Otherwise, I feel my inspiration escape into the air."

"Well, that can't happen," Claire says firmly. "Don't worry. I can wait."

I look down the hall toward the student government office. *Empty.* I give a big sigh of relief. "Let's go this way," I say.

Divinity meets us outside the office. I watch her expression carefully as we approach her to see if she might, somehow, still recognize "Sienna" from ChitChat. But Divinity's face shows no signs of recognition. A natural at public relations, she greets Claire with a smile and a quick handshake.

"I'm so sorry," Divinity begins. "This is not the best day to get a real sense of Fort Collins High School," she says, walking us toward the library. "Everyone is caught up in homecoming fever. There's no one around."

That's the idea.

We head down the deserted science hallway and out toward the choir room with Divinity narrating as we go. "These are the foreign languages classrooms . . . This is the theater area . . ."

Suddenly, the side doors pop open and Dezirea comes in with two other girls from the cheerleading squad, laughing and talking.

Dezirea.

My heart thuds.

Oh, no. No. No. No.

This wasn't supposed to happen. No one was supposed to be around.

If Dezirea sees "Sienna," it's all over.

I grab Claire's arm and yank her into the computer room.

"Hey," Claire says, rubbing her arm and staring at me like I'm crazy.

Dezirea and the other two girls pass by without noticing us. I let out a breath.

"What's going on?" Claire asks me, but I'm too shaken up to answer.

Divinity follows us into the computer room and gives me a curious look. "Why did you come in here?" she asks me.

"I thought Claire might be interested in our coding class, so just wanted to make sure she saw the computer lab," I invent. Lame, but it seems to work.

Divinity smiles and nods.

Claire looks bored, glancing around briefly. "So it pretty much looks like every other computer classroom," she says, and she's right.

I glance out the door toward the office. The hall is empty. "We're probably about finished here," I say, trying to hurry things along. "As you can see, there's nothing special about Fort Collins High School. It's probably a lot like your school, but without all your friends."

Divinity looks at me like I just stabbed her in the heart. "No way, Maisie. Fort Collins High is the best school in the world!"

She's the senior class president. She has to say that.

Divinity leads us back outside and out toward the senior lockers. I'm even more on edge than I was before, constantly checking over my shoulder in case Dezirea—or anyone else—should appear. We have to get out of here. Now.

Claire pauses to read the homecoming posters lining the windows. "It's so cool that Lexi Singh is coming to homecoming. And the cosplay masquerade theme is brilliant."

Divinity jumps on Claire's first positive reaction. "The theme was my idea," she says proudly. "And having Lexi actually *at* the dance?" She pauses and puts a hand over her heart. "That's a dream come true."

I agree with Divinity, but I'm too anxious to start talking about Lexi. I need to hustle Claire off school grounds before any other kids show up.

"Come on," I tell Claire, grabbing her arm and leading her ahead.

"Wait." Divinity stops suddenly and I bump into her back. "I have a great idea."

Claire and I look at her curiously.

"You could come to the dance this Friday night!" Divinity says to Claire with a big grin.

Noooooo. No. No. No.

"She can't do that." I make myself shake my head and look as sorry as possible. "Only students can attend."

"But I can give you an invitation," Divinity says helpfully. "We made up some special passes because it's homecoming, and I have a couple left. Then you can actually meet some people here and see what we're *really* like."

"Great idea." Claire beams at her.

I feel the panic bubbling up inside me. Divinity digs around in her backpack, then proudly hands over a blue cardstock invitation with the words COSPLAY MASQUERADE printed in silver letters at the top.

"Here you go," she says. "I hope to see you there."

"Me too." Claire puts the invitation in her purse. I can see the blue edge sticking out of the top, mocking me.

My stomach twists into a ball. I have to fix this. Now.

The line between lying and stealing is a thread. I cross it without another thought. When Claire hugs Divinity good-bye, I slip the invitation out of Claire's bag and slide it into my back pocket. Even if Claire shows up at the dance, she won't be able to get inside.

Outside, I lean against my car, watching Claire pull out of the parking lot, my hand on my pounding chest. My control is slipping away. This whole Sienna lie has gotten much bigger than I wanted.

I pull out the homecoming invitation from my pocket and tear it in half.

Who have I become? A hero or a villain?

CHITCHAT DIRECT MESSAGE

JESSE: CONGRATULATIONS!

SIENNA: ??

JESSE: YOU ARE TALKING TO THE SOPHOMORE HOMECOMING PRINCE.

JESSE: ← ME

SIENNA: WOW! I'VE ALWAYS WANTED TO KNOW A ROYAL.

JESSE: THERE'S A PARADE AFTER SCHOOL TOMORROW TO KICK OFF HOMECOMING WEEKEND. I'M ON THE FLOAT AND EVERYTHING.

SIENNA: IMPRESSIVE.

JESSE: I KNOW IT'S LAST MINUTE . . . *TAKING A DEEP BREATH*

JESSE: MAYBE YOU COULD COME AND BE UP THERE WITH ME? THERE WOULD BE A PLACE FOR YOU TO SIT BESIDE ME.

My heart races. This is where Sienna says no, Jesse is crushed, and Sienna disappears forever. The game is over.

JESSE: SAY SOMETHING. ANYTHING.

The dark side whispers in my ear.

This is an opportunity I never could have imagined. A parade. How much more public can you get? Even though I didn't know it was coming, it's the ending I need for this story. Jesse Santos's downfall will play out in front of the world, and everyone will finally see he's no better than the rest of us.

JESSE: ← THIS IS ME ASKING YOU OUT.

All my deception has led up to this one sentence typed across my screen. It should feel different. More triumphant.

SIENNA: LIKE A DATE?

JESSE: I WAS HOPING.

I can't believe I'm really going to do this, but it's time to see if he is telling the truth or just stringing me—I mean Sienna—along. It worked with Dezirea, and now it's time for the true test. I'm ready.

SIENNA: YES.

JESSE: SERIOUSLY????????

SIENNA: YES.

JESSE: IN REAL LIFE????

SIENNA: YES.

JESSE: AWESOME. ☺ I TOLD EVERYONE ABOUT YOU. MY
FRIENDS ARE EXCITED TO MEET YOU.

SIENNA: I'LL MEET YOU AT THE PARADE. CAN'T WAIT.

CHAPTER EIGHTEEN

On Thursday after school, Mountain Avenue and Mason Street are blocked off from traffic. People stream toward the parade route, carrying lawn chairs and blankets. Traffic officers direct everyone who's in the parade to the Mountain Avenue intersection, where the lineup is getting organized. Two teachers with huge badges hanging from their necks sit behind the table, patiently checking in parade participants.

I sit on a cold bench in a striped blue skirt listening to the sound of the band warming up—something with a lot of drums. The crisp wind tangles my hair around my face, but the sky is bright with not a sign of a cloud. The fall colors swirl around the street in clumps of orange, red, and yellow leaves. It's the kind of day that should smell like popcorn and pumpkins. My skirt is too short and I tug the hem of it down toward my knees for the fiftieth time, looking around nervously. But everyone is focused on getting ready for the start of the parade and couldn't care less if I'm there or not.

Behind the school banner that signals the start of the parade, the cheerleading squad warms up their routine, stepping and spinning on the street. Camila barks orders like a drill sergeant and the girls respond with perfect synchronization, pom-poms shaking enthusiastically. My phone buzzes in my lap.

GRACE: WE'RE DOWN AT THE CORNER OF OLIVE. SAVING YOU A PLACE.

ME: OK. RUNNING LATE. BE THERE SOON.

Lies come so easy to me now.

Two giggling girls pass my bench, a cloud of competing perfumes trailing behind them. They wear matching Catwoman costumes and high, spiky heels instead of their sweaters and jeans from earlier in the day. Three band boys hang out under the trees on the far side of the street, heads bowed over the screens in their hands. The girls' greeting is the only thing that makes them look up. Together they head off farther down the route to get a good seat for the show.

Behind the final row of drums in the band is a line of cars decorated with hand-lettered posters. The red mustang convertible near the end is completely covered with life-sized Nosy Parker cutouts and bright blue streamers. The sign on the driver's-side door says LEXI SINGH, announcing proudly who will soon be sitting in the back seat waving to the crowd. Normally, that's what I'd be focused on—waiting to see Lexi sitting in the car and hoping she would wave in my direction. But all my attention is on the final float in the parade, a flatbed trailer pulled behind a big orange tractor. The culminating masterpiece of the annual homecoming parade, the decorations have grown more gaudy and ostentatious with each group of seniors eager to outdo the last. Two huge, oversized gold thrones sit up on a raised platform for the homecoming king and queen. To the right of each throne is a smaller, undecorated chair for their escorts. On the lower level, twelve similar, slightly smaller thrones and chairs sit waiting for the court.

A group gathers around the front of the float, beside the tractor and directly in front of me. Divinity, who is homecoming queen, and her escort, William, talk to the junior homecoming prince, Sean Grier, and his escort and longtime girlfriend, Brie Knight. Then Jesse walks up to the group, wearing a crisp white button-down shirt and jeans. In one hand he holds a bouquet of roses tied with a glittery gold bow. I can feel the thorns piercing my heart from here.

While I watch, Jesse throws back his head and laughs at something the freshman homecoming prince says to him. I realize I've never really seen him laugh in such a *genuine* way. Smarmy smiles? Definitely. Gut-busting laughter? Rarely. The sight of him, face lit up with sheer joy, gives me a strange little pang I want to immediately dismiss. He won't be laughing for long.

The band director shouts out directions, and the flute players sitting on the curb stand up and get back in line. Jesse checks his phone several times and watches the stream of people passing. Several people congratulate him, slapping his back and high-fiving. As the music cranks up, he stands, walking up and down in front of the trailer.

The dance team takes a break and Dezirea heads over to the float, dragging Graham along beside her. Her short flared skirt shows off her toned brown legs perfectly. Bella and Hunter follow closely.

"Why aren't you up there already, Prince Jesse?" Dezirea asks.

"More importantly, where is this girl we've heard all about?" Bella demands. She wears her hair in a fishtail braid I know took her an extra hour of prep time. The bright red sweater over her cheerleading uniform is totally nonregulation, and she claps her mitten-covered hands together periodically as though they are freezing.

"She'll be here," Jesse says confidently.

My heart sinks. This is harder to watch than I expected.

"She's driving up from Denver. Might have hit traffic," he adds, glancing around at the crowd. I sink a little farther down on the bench.

"Uh-huh," Hunter says, like he totally doesn't believe it. "Probably *imaginary* traffic."

Bella giggles. Graham shoots him a look, but Hunter's just getting started. "Who'd have thought Prince Charming would end up being the biggest loser today?"

Bella boos loudly and Graham joins in, cupping his hands around his mouth to intensify the sound.

"Photo op," Dezirea says, obviously trying to change the mood. They pose and snap pictures, pulling a reluctant Jesse into the group shot. They take another. Then one more. The group gets restless, and finally Dezirea and Graham step up to take their places, waving good-bye. The king and queen ascend to their thrones, handing bouquets of roses to their respective dates.

"Are you getting up there or not?" Bella looks back and forth from the float to Jesse.

"Look," Hunter says, putting his arm around Jesse's shoulders. "I can pick someone out of the crowd for you. Sort of like a placeholder. There are plenty of girls dying to be beside you."

Jesse shakes his head. "I'm going to wait down here a few more minutes."

"Dude," Hunter tells him. "Face it. Mystery girl is not coming."

"Maybe not, but I'm still going to wait for her."

Hunter shrugs and leaves him. "Whatever," he says, and then he and Bella head down the side of the street toward the start of the parade route.

Casey Austin, the drum major, steps up front and signals the start of the parade. The drum line—three snare drums, two bass drums, and a set of cymbals—keep everyone in step as they start to move down the street. I watch the trumpets in their blue tunics decorated with gold braids and tall hats. Jesse was right. No football players in helmets and pads.

Everyone but Jesse is on the float, dates in place holding their bouquets. Only two places are empty. His phone is out in his hand where he can see it constantly, and he paces back and forth quicker with each turn. Every so often, he looks up and scans the street, and each time he does, I sink deeper onto the bench. Finally, his shoulders sag and he steps up on the float. He briefly taps at his phone before climbing up farther to take his place. He lays the bouquet of roses on the empty chair beside him, saving a spot for someone who is never going to come. My phone vibrates in my pocket.

It's a ChitChat message for Sienna.

JESSE: DID WE GET OUR WIRES CROSSED? ARE YOU RUNNING LATE?

My brain is on fire. This moment should feel so right, so beautiful. This is why I created Sienna. So why am I feeling so sorry for him?

I don't respond. I put my phone away.

The band reaches the middle of the next block and they break into the fight song, trumpet players swinging left, right, up, and down in perfect rhythm, just missing the heads of their fellow bandmates. The crowd along the route starts to sing along, chanting with raised fists.

I slip off the bench and through the crowd, overwhelmed by the image of Jesse's face and that wistful, hopeful look as he scans the crowd looking for . . . me. *But not me.*

My plan to manipulate Jesse into falling for Sienna worked. Now she's hurt him. But I don't feel happy about it. Just the opposite. This is not like a two-dimensional sketch with characters I can control. These are real people with real feelings. My shape-shifting is cruelly complete. I have become something different.

A fraud.

A liar.

A fake.

I press my lips together tight. I have to end this now, before it goes any further.

CHITCHAT DIRECT MESSAGE

JESSE: SIENNA? WHERE WERE YOU? WHY DIDN'T YOU
SHOW UP?

JESSE: HELLO?

CHAPTER NINETEEN

I created a monster and her name is Sienna. She has to go away. The plan is simple. Sienna can disappear and this whole world I've created can disappear, too. Of course, Dezirea will be sad. And Jesse? I don't want to think about it. It will be the end to a great adventure. I was in control when it started, and now I will create the ending. The story isn't turning out the way I intended.

That night, I scan through the fake accounts I created, my foot jiggling nervously under the desk. Brittany, Sienna's bestie—the girl whose face I took from the acne cream ad—has the most comments on Sienna's posts. I log off of Sienna's profile and log on as Brittany.

BRITTANY: SO WORRIED ABOUT MY FRIEND SIENNA!! SHE WAS IN A CAR WRECK YESTERDAY AFTER SCHOOL. EVERYBODY KEEP HER IN YOUR THOUGHTS AND PRAYERS.

I tag Sienna on the post so Jesse and Dezirea are sure to see it, then spend the next hour logging in and out of all my imaginary Sienna friend accounts to post various messages of support on Sienna's page. My heart is beating crazy fast, but I tell myself this is what I have to do.

Around and around we go. Where we stop no one knows.

Of course I feel guilty, but it's better Sienna goes away now before things get even more complicated. She's not going to die or anything that serious. Because that would just be cruel. And horrible. And I'm not a cruel and horrible person.

Am I?

I log out of ChitChat and shut down my computer before I can change my mind. Sienna is gone. I squeeze my eyes tight. The mystery of what happened to her might linger for a while, but people have short attention spans. They will move on to the next drama—one that doesn't involve me. There is no excuse now.

I try to distract myself by drawing a *Froot Loops* sketch. In this one, I change into a fly. A fly might not be particularly glamorous in the shape-shifting world, but tonight I feel like a fly on the walls of Fort Collins High School. I see everything, just sitting there, watching and listening. Unfortunately, flies are also attracted by garbage—the worst of people's drama and the smelliest of conflicts. Most of the time, people don't even see the fly. The last frame sits empty, but I can't think of a way to end it. There is nothing triumphant and redeeming about this story. It is just sad.

When I turn out the lights and stare up at the ceiling, I can think of nothing else. Sienna is becoming too real.

And worst of all, Jesse and Dezirea are becoming real, too. I know things now that make me see them differently. Like Dezirea's dreams of still wanting to be a ballerina. And that Jesse spends every weekend rocking tiny babies to sleep. No one is the way I drew them—one-dimensional and shallow. Nothing is simply black and white anymore. My alternative world has exploded with colors I never knew existed.

There is a soft thud on the end of the bed and Katy Purry stalks up the covers toward my chest. She curls up, not quite touching my side, and begins to lick the fur on her fluffy black tail as though I don't exist. Finally, I get up, earning an outraged glare from a displaced Katy Purry, and dig my earbuds out of my backpack. I plug them into my phone and hit *play*. By the time the trumpet starts to play, tears are streaming down my face and soaking my pillow. I close my eyes and listen to the sound of my lonely heart.

"You lie awake and think about the boy."

CHITCHAT DIRECT MESSAGE

DEZIREA: HI SIENNA. ARE YOU OKAY?

DEZIREA: I SAW YOU WERE IN AN ACCIDENT. I'M THINKING OF YOU. ☹

CHITCHAT DIRECT MESSAGE

JESSE: I'M SORRY I WAS ANGRY ABOUT THE PARADE.

JESSE: I DIDN'T KNOW ABOUT THE ACCIDENT.

JESSE: PLEASE LET ME KNOW YOU'RE ALL RIGHT.

JESSE: PLEASE?

JESSE: CALL ME. TEXT ME. SOMETHING???

CHAPTER TWENTY

On Friday morning, Jesse seems distracted. His eyes are red rimmed and he looks exhausted. I don't say anything about the parade, but there was a buzz in the hallways this morning about the empty seat beside him. The rumor is he was stood up by his online girlfriend, and his unsettled appearance this morning is only adding fuel to the fire.

"You okay?" I ask, but I think I know. He's not.

He shrugs. "Just worried about a friend."

"Who?"

"You don't know her."

But I do.

"What happened to her?"

"A car accident."

I wait, a hollow smile pasted on my face. The guilt is so sharp I can hardly breathe. *This is for the best.* "Is she going to be okay?" I ask, because I think I should.

His jaw is set hard and there is a tiny pulse in his cheek. "I don't know."

"Is it the girl you were telling me about? The one online?"

He nods. His eyes are so broken. All the breath goes out of my lungs. I feel an almost-irresistible urge to comfort him. *Isn't this exactly what I wanted?* Then why does it feel so bad?

I blink a couple of times and fiddle with the pipette in front of us. Silence falls for a few seconds, and then I say, "I'm sure she's fine. You'll probably hear from her soon."

He looks down at the table and shakes his head.

Pull it together, I tell myself.

I bite a nail, rearrange the papers in front of us, and try to look as casual as possible. "Have you ever done anything really bad to someone?" I suddenly ask. "And you don't know how to fix it?"

"Yes," he says. "Everyone messes up sometime."

"I'm talking *really* bad."

"Look who you're talking to." He grins at me, and a glimmer of the old Jesse comes through loud and clear. "In case you don't know it, I can be a real jerk sometimes."

"No. Really?" I act shocked.

"I know it sounds lame, but sometimes it helps to say you're sorry," he says. "When you really mean it."

"Yeah," I say, rinsing out the beaker. "Thanks."

Camila suddenly appears at Jesse's side and we both jump. "Oh. My. God. I just heard," she squeals.

"What?" Jesse asks.

"You tried out for band? Tell me it's not true. Jesse Santos, band geek?" She punches his shoulder playfully.

Jesse smiles proudly. "I didn't just *try out*," he says. "I *made* the band. I start right after football season ends."

I stare at him. My heart fills with some kind of wonder. I helped make this happen. Well, *Sienna* made this happen. But still. She—I—gave Jesse the confidence to go for his dream. Maybe everything I've done hasn't been all bad.

Camila clasps her hands to her heart. "Next thing you know you'll be marching at halftime."

"Would if I could," Jesse says smugly.

Camila laughs and walks away, and my thoughts return to Sienna's "accident" and all the lies. I manage to avoid saying anything else to Jesse for the rest of the class.

⌖ ⌖ ⌖

I meet Grace and Owen after class outside the chemistry lab. I barely manage a nod, my mind still on my conversation with Jesse.

"So we'll pick you up for the game at about five?" Grace asks.

"I'm not going to the game," I say.

"Then we'll swing by and pick you up afterward for the dance," Owen says. "My dad said I can use his car."

"I don't know," I say. "I thought the two of you are going together."

Grace looks confused. "We are. But you're going with us, too. It's already decided."

"You have to go to the dance," Owen says. "Lexi's going to be there, and you might get the opportunity to meet her face-to-face."

He's right. I have to go. If I don't, I'll never have the chance to meet Lexi. She's my ticket out of all this mess I've created. Once I'm her protégé, everything will work out somehow.

"Okay," I say. "But I'll drive myself and meet you guys there."

Owen nods. "Cool."

"What are you going to be?" I ask.

"Ant-Man and the Wasp," Owen says proudly. He winks at me.

"What did you decide on?" Grace asks me.

"I'm not sure yet." But I know one thing. I won't be myself.

CLAIRE: HEY MAISIE! SO I'M THINKING I MIGHT COME UP FOR THE DANCE. CAN'T FIND THE INVITATION, THOUGH.

CLAIRE: CAN YOU GET ME ANOTHER ONE?

CLAIRE: OR GET ME IN?

CLAIRE: HELLO?

CHAPTER TWENTY-ONE

The cosplay masquerade ball is a huge hit. The gym is decorated with purple balloons and streamers. Green floodlights illuminate the walls with a ghostly glow, giving the impression of some underground hideout for all the superheroes in attendance. And the costumes are the main focus. Everyone enthusiastically supported the theme.

A couple of stormtroopers hang out by the double doors with Archie and Veronica. Spock and Superman dance together by the refreshment table. Not surprisingly, I immediately spot at least four versions of Nosy Parker. Two are wearing Nosy's plaid school uniform with her signature pearls. The other two dress in sleek black gowns with high heels and huge sunglasses—Nosy when she's dressed up. Bella is impressive as Mystique in her blue body suit and blue face paint. Dezirea is an ultra cool Jessica Jones, complete with a camera strapped around her neck, buckled motorcycle boots, and a black leather jacket.

A DJ is playing music on the stage at the far end of the room. In front of him, a small cluster of enthusiastic dancers are jumping around to a fast song, hands waving wildly in the air.

When I was a child, I loved costumes. Veronica and I went all out every Halloween, making elaborate costumes based on our favorite characters. My sister was usually a flavor-of-the-month kind of princess, but I always went for the darker side. Even then, monsters, villians, and vicious beasts were much more my style.

Tonight, a Catwoman mask covers the top half of my face, and the rest of my body is cloaked in a loose black top, black jeans, and black boots: an easy costume to gather together from my closet. I relax a tiny bit behind the security of the mask, following Ant-Man and the Wasp— Owen and Grace—through the crowd. The costume gives me the illusion of making my very visible body a little more invisible.

My eyes adjust to the dark and I see the football team make their way into the gym to the accompaniment of cheers and high fives. Our team won by two touchdowns, and everyone is in the mood to celebrate. The team's group costume is simple—they each wear Superman capes with a big red *S* taped on the front of their blue T-shirts. I know Jesse is there among them but I look away before I can see him.

The music slows and some dancers leave the floor. Others partner up. Dezirea runs up to Graham and gives him a quick kiss, then links her arm through his to pull him out on the dance floor.

"Do you want to dance?" Grace asks Owen. He nods and they leave, hand in hand.

I move into the shadows, my back pressed flat against the wall. I watch as the Wasp wraps her arms around Ant-Man's neck and they slowly sway to the music. My throat gets tight and it feels like I'm standing outside looking in the window of a fancy restaurant—drooling and hungry. I look away.

Jesse stands nearby in his Superman cape, his silver homecoming prince crown dangling from one hand. He's almost close enough to touch if I were to step toward him, yet there's so much space between us. We're a million miles apart.

A winner's glow lights up his face, erasing all the troubled signs from this morning. He shoulders his way through the crowd, bumping fists and accepting congratulations for tonight's victory. Everybody adores him—from the way he smiles to the way he moves across the room. My dark side whispers in my ear and, for a minute, I feel a seething rage at how oblivious he is to my revenge. I put my heart and soul into my charade and he walks through the room untouched.

Was it worth it?

I swallow hard. It's bittersweet. I stand there like a rock in the middle of a white-water river—the bubbling excitement of the crowd a contrast to my mood.

"There you are." Grace stands in front of me with Owen. "We've been looking for you."

"I blend in," I say, wishing it were true but knowing it never will be.

"They're going to make the announcement," Owen says, his eyes on the stage.

The homecoming king, Josiah Brown, adjusts his gold foil crown on his head and steps up to the microphone. He taps at it a couple of times and someone stops the music. The excited roar of the crowd lessens to a rumble.

Josiah leans down from his six-foot-plus height to reach the mic stand. "Hello out there!" he says in his best news anchor voice. "I know you guys are not here tonight to see me."

There is scattered laughter. Someone shouts from the back of the room, "You know it!" And there is more laughter.

Josiah quiets the rowdy crowd again, then continues, "But I'm the lucky one who gets to introduce our guest of honor. Help me welcome our most famous graduate ever . . ."

The DJ plays a drumroll and the crowd draws in one big collective breath.

Oh my God. Somehow I forgot all about Lexi. But it's really happening. She's here!

Josiah shouts into the microphone, "Lexi Singh!"

When Lexi appears onstage, everyone erupts into cheers. In person, she is larger than life even though she is only five feet tall. Her thick black hair is pulled up into a high ponytail that swishes from side to side as she walks toward the microphone. She wears cute peg pants in a black-and-white check paired with a black turtleneck and black high-top Converse All Stars. Everything about her is perfect. I clap as hard as I can.

Lexi bounces up to the microphone, grins widely, and holds up her hands to quiet the noise. The silence is almost immediate.

"I want to thank everyone for coming out this evening. It's so great to be back home in Fort Collins." She beams at the audience.

Cheers again.

"You all look great," Lexi says, then laughs at the enthusiastic response. "I'm ready to meet my special mentees back here in the coach's office in thirty minutes. And don't be late!"

She motions to the door at the back of the gym. I wait, a nervous smile on my lips. The floor stretches in front of me like a huge crevasse and I am so close to falling, I lean against the wall for support. I want this so bad I can hardly breathe.

Lexi goes on. "I loved watching all those ChitChat videos. Didn't you?"

That gets a big round of applause from even the students who didn't turn in videos.

"It was so hard to choose the winners. We have three." Lexi holds up three fingers for emphasis. There is a collective gasp across the room and I can almost see everyone scoot forward a step toward the stage. "And I really wish it could have been more."

My heart is pounding and my palms are clammy. *This is it.*

"The first winner is your amazing senior class president,

Divinity Gates." There is a burst of applause and I hear Divinity shriek with joy. Lexi holds one hand over her eyes and peers into the lights. "I can't wait to talk to you, Divinity."

"Same here!" Divinity yells back. Everyone laughs.

Lexi checks her phone. "Next is . . . Dezirea Davis."

Squeals of delight ring out from the corner. I turn around to see Dezirea hugging Bella. I'm happy for her. She deserves it.

"And last but certainly not least . . ." Lexi pauses.

Grace reaches for my hand and squeezes it tight.

"Another sophomore . . ."

I breathe. My heart beats. But I'm not inside my body anymore.

"Maisie Fernandez."

I feel my eyes go wide. I can't believe it. Lexi really said my name.

"It's you, Maisie!" Grace says, grabbing me in a hug.

I forget all about Jesse and Sienna. Grace and I jump up and down, screaming and hugging each other. My heart pounds rapid and crazy. It's a life-changing moment.

Like fate.

CHAPTER TWENTY-TWO

When I get back to the coach's office, a girl with outrageously, no-way-it-is-possibly-real red hair looks at me. Her badge says HELLO! MY NAME IS SUMMER in big blue letters. She is holding a clipboard and has a Bluetooth earpiece that she taps at periodically.

"Are you Maisie?" Summer asks me.

I nod, pulling the Catwoman mask off so she can see me better.

"I'm Lexi's assistant." She looks at her list, then back at me. "It says here that Lexi wants to talk to you."

I nod again, enthusiastically.

"Why don't you have a seat?" Summer motions toward a couple of empty chairs by the door and taps at her earpiece. "Lexi's with . . ." She looks down at her clipboard. "Divinity right now, but you're up next."

I perch carefully on the chair, biting my lower lip nervously. There's no sign of Dezirea yet.

Divinity comes out of the office, grinning widely, and Summer waves me in.

"Your turn," she says with a perky fake smile.

I stumble toward the office door, my brain in a fog. I've

dreamed of this happening so many times. My heart is going fast and loud. Is this real?

Lexi sits at the tiny desk across from the door. She looks up when I enter and smiles. It's like a spotlight is shining down on her thick black hair, illuminating her brilliance. This is my chance. Now or never. I make my way forward. Then I'm there, standing in front of her.

"Hey," she says, looking up at me. "I'm Lexi."

"I—I know," I stammer. I don't know whether I'm scared, or nervous, or just plain terrified. But there's no going back now.

"Come over and sit down." She motions to the chair across from her. I manage to take the few steps and perch on the edge of the seat.

I gather my courage and find my voice. "My name is Maisie and I want to draw."

Duh. It sounds stupid. So simplistic.

"Cool." Lexi's smile is warm and inviting. "Yes, I remember the comic strip you showed in your ChitChat video. I'd like to see some more of your work."

She remembers!

"Um. Sure." I pull my phone out of my back pocket and pull up one of my drawings. It's a sketch of Dezirea at her party. "You can scroll from here. This is my album of drawings on my phone." Lexi takes my phone and acts like she doesn't notice my shaking hands.

Lexi studies the first drawing, her brows furrowing. I wait. Her fingers magnify the image quickly. Then she slides her finger around on the screen to look at every angle. More silence. Finally she looks up and meets my eyes.

"Do you really want to know what I think?" she asks matter-of-factly.

I take a deep breath and let it out slowly, nodding. I can hardly choke out the answer. "More than anything."

"Do you really want my opinion, or for me to just say something nice?"

"I want to know the truth."

Lexi nods, pushing her black hair over one shoulder. She looks from the drawing back to me.

"You're very talented."

The relief is intense. She likes it.

Lexi Singh thinks I'm talented.

My hands are still shaking, but now I'm smiling.

I wait while Lexi scrolls through a few more of my pictures. A minute passes. Then a few more. Her face gives nothing away. "Can you work with a variety of graphic software, such as Adobe's Photoshop and Illustrator, and Made With Mischief?" she asks.

I nod.

"A Wacom tablet is also a must-have."

"Thanks for the tip," I say.

"Do you have a personal website?"

I shake my head.

"You need one. But I'd also suggest you take a look at some other sites like Reddit, Imgur, Tapas, or Webtoon, just to name a few. Find other people who share your passion and study what they do."

"Thanks," I say again. This advice is awesome.

Finally, Lexi looks up and clears her throat. "You're really good. I see a lot of myself in your work."

My head buzzes. This is everything I've been dreaming of hearing. I can't believe it.

"I . . . wow," I manage to say. "Thank you. That means so much."

"But . . ." Her voice trails off and my world ends. Panic freezes the smile on my face.

"I don't see *you*."

What?

My expression must show how confused I feel.

Lexi takes a deep breath and puts her palms down on the table in between us, leaning in to look straight into my eyes.

"Do you want to do this?" Lexi asks.

I nod. "I can't see myself doing anything else."

"Then listen. The things you've shown me are good, but they are not good enough."

The walls of my dream start to crumble before my eyes.

"I think you're incredibly talented, but you need to dig deeper," Lexi goes on. "Find your own voice. Your own style."

I try to say "okay," but no sound comes out.

"When an artist goes out into the world, she doesn't see things the same way as everyone else. It's that difference—that uniqueness—that matters. And in that uniqueness is a deep truth." Lexi pauses. "I don't see that truth in your drawings. Not here." She taps my phone. "Not yet."

There are tears in my eyes. I blink and they roll down my cheeks. There is no use in wiping them away.

"Truth?" I whisper.

Lexi nods. "I want to see what's true. Be yourself. Nobody else can."

I'm not even embarrassed that Lexi Singh sees me crying. I just mumble thank you, take my phone back from her, and get to my feet. I don't remember stumbling back into the crowded gym, almost bumping into Dezirea, who's waiting at the door to come inside.

Lexi Singh doesn't think I'm good enough.

I'm not enough. It's over for me. My dream is dead.

CHAPTER TWENTY-THREE

My brain feels fuzzy and disconnected from my body. Music and people surround me, but I'm standing all alone in a bubble of disappointment. I showed Lexi what I was capable of, but she didn't like my drawings. All I can think of are her comments. So cruel and cutting. She said she didn't see truth in my drawings. Maybe she's right. Maybe I am a fake.

The string of lights draped across the basketball goals glow into life for a slow song. People mill around the dancing couples, talking and laughing. I lurk in the back behind a group of theater kids, desperately wanting to leave, but seeing no sign of Ant-Man or the Wasp.

I see Dezirea and Camila chattering away over by the refreshment table. Dezirea does a quick twirl and I can tell she's happy about her conversation with Lexi. If I were Sienna, I would congratulate her. Instead, I just watch her slip an arm through Camila's and say something that makes them both throw back their heads and laugh. They start toward the bleachers, blowing kisses into the air over their shoulders like true stars.

I guess it's good someone is happy about something. I stumble toward the door to the hallway, my thoughts a jumble of disappointment. Forget finding Owen and Grace. Maybe I should just go home. The night can't get any worse from here.

"Maisie!"

I look up at the shout. At the door is an all-too-familiar face.

Claire.

She waves me over excitedly. "Oh. My. God. So . . . this dance is amazing! I heard you were picked to meet Lexi Singh."

In shock, I just go into her open arms and let her do her hug thing. It is useless to resist. "How did you get in?" I mumble.

She holds me at arm's length and peers into my face. "I found Divinity on ChitChat and sent her a message. She left an extra pass for me at the door. Can you believe it?"

I look at Claire—Sienna—no, Claire. And all my schemes suddenly seem so stupid. My creation is in front of me, but she isn't me at all. No amount of spite, desire, or loneliness can justify what I've done. I can't even remember what is good anymore. I want to tell Claire to leave, to hide, to run away. But I can't move my mouth.

And then things get even worse.

"Sienna!"

My head jerks around. Jesse is walking toward me, waving. He is smiling, but he isn't looking at me.

He's looking at Claire.

My heart starts hammering and my stomach clenches. There is no way this will end up okay. Jesse isn't looking in my direction and I think I can probably slip out the door before he notices me. But then I see his face, his eyes wide and stunned, staring across the room. He looks surprised, but happy.

Everything is wrong, especially me.

Stay where you are, I think, as if I can send a silent message to Jesse. *Don't come any closer.*

But he keeps approaching Claire.

I want to jump in between the two of them and stop everything from happening. Instead, I watch him bridge the distance and get closer to Claire. The whole scene seems to be moving in wobbly slow motion, but I can't stop watching.

"Sienna?" The sound of his voice makes me feel ill. "What are you doing here?"

Claire looks at him with raised eyebrows and a vague smile. "Sorry?"

Jesse's grin wavers. "Are you kidding? It's me. Jesse."

Claire squints at him. "I don't know you."

Jesse frowns. "What's going on?" For the first time, he glances at me. "Do you know Maisie?" he asks Claire, looking back and forth at both of us.

So many questions. So much confusion. I need to leave now. Get out of here. But it's too late.

"Of course I know Maisie," Claire says. "But I don't know *you*."

Jesse shakes his head slowly, then rakes a hand through his hair in frustration.

"I don't get it," Jesse says to Claire. "We've been talking on ChitChat."

Claire shakes her head while I remain frozen. "No we haven't. You must have me confused with someone else."

There's a moment of silence and then Jesse's eyes lock on mine, his square-cut jaw tight. He's starting to piece things together. A crack shoots through my chest. I should feel guilty, but instead I just feel panic crashing over me so hard I want to scream. My mind desperately scrambles for a way out, but every path my brain follows ends up going off a cliff. Happy endings in this story don't exist.

I stand there beside Jesse and Claire, but it's like I am far away down a long dark tunnel. Their voices blur into incomprehensible sounds. I hear Claire's confusion as she says something else to Jesse. He says something back, then shakes his head slowly, pulling his phone out of his pocket. He taps on the screen and holds the phone out for her to see. The conversation continues, more animated and more intense. They are talking about me.

Saying horrible things.

True things.

Claire looks up at Jesse. Then they both look at me. Suddenly, they stop talking. Claire points at me, her hand shaking, and it's like her finger keeps me frozen in place. "You posted my pictures . . . as you?" Her face crumples. "How could you?"

I glance at Jesse, and his face looks stricken. "It was you the whole time," he says quietly.

Suddenly, Camila is there, and then Hunter . . . and Graham . . . and Dezirea. They are all listening and talking to Claire, to Jesse.

The story . . . my story . . . is spreading across the gym like wildfire. People are staring and pointing. *At me.*

My whole house of lies crashes down around me, the pain and panic ricocheting through my body. I have no one to blame but myself. I turn and run. I'm not sure where I'm going, but I have to leave.

My phone buzzes in my pocket. Then buzzes again. And again. But I don't stop to look. I dash out of the school and into the cold night. Finally, I reach the student parking lot. I find my car, slide into the driver's seat, and slam the door behind me, slumping down behind the wheel. It feels safe and hidden. Like my life used to be before I ruined everything. My hands tremble on the wheel and I try to catch my breath. I sit there, back in my old skin. I thought of my body as a horrible disguise, with my real self hidden somewhere inside, somewhere no one could see. The truth is my body is me. I'm not a shape-shifter or a superhero.

I'm just a super freak.

CHAPTER TWENTY-FOUR

I start driving without thinking of where I should go. Where can I go? I'm not ready to go home yet. I'm alone, and it's all my fault. My pain is mine. No one caused it but me. I want someone who knows me to tell me I'm okay. *Only I'm not.*

I drive to the only place I can think of—the Thinking Bench. Owen stands there, almost like he's been waiting for me.

I park my car, then get out and walk over to Owen.

"Where's Grace?" I ask him.

"She's still inside," he replies. "I told her I wanted to talk to you alone."

I swallow hard.

"Shall we sit down?" he asks formally.

"Yes." I brace myself, and then I sit down on the bench.

He sits beside me, then sighs a disappointed kind of sigh that hurts my heart. I wait for him to say something first. He finally does, and it's worse than I imagined.

"I heard a horrible rumor from some of the people at the dance. Is it true?"

He knows what I've done.

Everyone knows.

I nod.

"Tell me. I need to hear it all from you."

"I wanted to make Jesse understand what it felt like to be the butt of everyone's jokes, so I created the perfect girl online and made him fall for her," I say quickly. I've never admitted it out loud before. I exhale and look up at Owen.

"Really, Maisie?" he asks quietly. "It doesn't even sound like something you'd do." It's the first time I've ever seen him upset. Especially at me. His hands clench at his side into fists. His silence is like a knife in my chest.

"I can explain," I say, even though I really can't.

"Okay," he says, waiting.

"It wasn't the same for you," I tell him, my face flushing. "The whole Froot Loop thing? You just laughed it off. But I didn't think it was funny. It only made me angrier and angrier. There was nowhere for that anger to go, except into this . . . plan."

"Plan," Owen echoes, shaking his head.

I sigh. "I just wanted to be normal . . ."

"Normal?" Owen asks with a bite in his voice. "But we're *not* normal, Maisie. We've never been normal. Don't you get it? That's what we're good at. *Not. Being. Normal.*"

Lexi's voice echoes in my brain. *Be yourself. Nobody else can.*

I think back to Claire and Jesse and Dezirea and all the people at the dance. Pointing at me and staring. I put my head in my hands and groan.

"Everyone hates me now," I say.

Owen is silent, and I glance up at him.

Owen tilts his head, his eyes narrowing. "Not everyone," he says softly. "I don't."

"You should." My eyes fill up with tears. I don't deserve him.

"I know who you are inside and outside. And I like both." He leans in to my shoulder just a tiny bit, but the slightest of touches means the world to me. "Even when you do really stupid things."

Relief floods over me. Owen is still here and he's still going to tell me the truth. Somehow I didn't screw this— our friendship—up. At least, I hope not.

"Thank you," I say, starting to sob so hard my shoulders shake.

"You don't need to cry," Owen says. But he lets me. After a while, I can talk again.

"Lexi Singh didn't like my pictures," I sniffle. "She said I need to dig deeper and be more honest."

"That's an understatement," Owen says dryly.

"I can't even draw myself."

"Because you don't see yourself."

I wipe the tears away from my face. "Owen, listen. You know that I don't fit into a world where girls have to look a certain way. I'll never look like Sienna or Dezirea or Camila—or any of the other girls who everyone calls pretty."

Owen holds up a hand, interrupting me. "Wait. Who's Sienna?"

Right. I sort of assumed Owen would have heard her name amid the rumors. "She's the girl I made up online. Using Claire's photos." Saying the words out loud makes my throat tighten.

"Oh," Owen says quietly. "Okay."

We're silent for a minute and then Owen speaks again.

"So maybe you don't look like those girls," he says, "but they will never see the world from your eyes. You have to show what *you* see to them, and everyone else. You're the only one who can."

I nod.

"I wanted to give you something." Owen reaches into his pocket and pulls out a drawing. It's a *Froot Loops* strip where he shape-shifts into a crow. He holds it out to me, but I can't take it from him. He lets the slip of paper go and it drifts down to the ground like a tiny airplane. I watch it land and my eyes fill up again.

"Why did you bring this tonight?" I ask.

"It's an amazing picture. I thought you might want to show it to Lexi."

"I showed her my drawings that looked most like *her* style—realistic, clean, and sophisticated. I didn't show her this stuff."

"Maybe you should have."

"You're right," I say, starting to tear up again. What would I do without Owen? I am so grateful that he didn't give up on me after he found out what I did. "Our friendship is the best friendship I've ever had," I blurt out, looking at him. "I can't lose you."

"Just because we're best friends doesn't mean we can't have more friends." We both know he's talking about Grace. "Gaining something doesn't mean you have to lose something in return. Sometimes our hearts just get bigger."

"Where did you learn that?" I sniffle.

"Hygge."

I bite my lower lip and shake my head in confusion. "What?"

"It's my next self-study," Owen says.

"Honestly, I'm glad we're moving away from humor, but what is . . ." I don't even know how to repeat the word. "That?"

"It's Danish and the word doesn't transfer exactly into English, but it sort of means coziness," Owen says. "It's all about comfort, warmth, and togetherness."

"Then I need some hygge." I lean my head on his shoulder.

He pats the top of my head awkwardly with one hand. "We all do."

Owen is incredibly profound sometimes.

☞　☞　☞

As soon as I get home, I open ChitChat as Sienna and the response is overwhelming. The story of my deception not only spread throughout the dance, but also blasted through the internet with lightning speed. Sienna's wall is covered with messages from random people I don't even know.

DON'T FOLLOW HER. SHE'S A FAKE!!!!

I don't want to keep looking, but I can't stop.

WARNING! THIS IS A FAKE ACCOUNT.

But it gets worse. Now the notices are on my own account, too. People have connected Sienna to me and they are blasting the news to anyone who will listen.

THIS GIRL IS A CREEPER! DON'T FOLLOW HER.

GET YOUR OWN LIFE AND STOP TRYING TO STEAL OTHER PEOPLE'S YOU FAT COW.

My throat constricts. I feel every comment like a cut across my skin. Especially the ones from the people I know.

CAMILA: YOU ARE SO SAD. DO YOU HATE YOURSELF THAT MUCH?

BELLA: SHE'S JUST A LONELY LOSER. SO CRAZY SHE HAS TO FAKE HER OWN FACE!

I make myself click over to Claire's profile. She's just posted something new.

CLAIRE: PLEASE READ! DON'T CONTACT OR
COMMUNICATE WITH SIENNA MARAS. SHE IS
PRETENDING TO BE ME!! SHE IS A LIAR.

I can't blame her. She's right. I am a liar. I keep reading. It is my punishment, and I deserve every word.

CLAIRE: SHE EVEN SAID I WAS IN A CAR ACCIDENT! SO
SICK.

Immediately, people rally to Claire's side.

OMG! THIS IS SOOOOOOO WEIRD! YOU SHOULD REPORT
HER. SHARING RIGHT NOW!

YOU DON'T DESERVE THIS! I'M SO SORRY THIS IS
HAPPENING TO YOU.

There are no comments or updates from Dezirea, or from Jesse. I don't know if I feel relieved or sad about that.

CHAPTER TWENTY-FIVE

Sienna is gone. I deleted her profile from ChitChat, but not before the comments started pouring in. After I finish reading through them all, I cry. Sobbing, gasping, wrenching crying like I haven't done since I was a child. The kind of crying that leaves me gasping for breath. When the tears eventually slow, my head aches.

Finally, I can't cry anymore. I curl into a tight circle and pull up the covers. Katy Purry tucks tightly into the crook of my knee and I reach for my sketchbook. I draw a square on the paper—a frame. I imagine putting my bitterness, anger, and hatred of myself into that frame. The pencil flies across the page as I scribble black lines circling down down down into the blackness of the box. I close my eyes. When I open them again, I turn the pencil over and I erase everything. I let it go. The blankness of the paper is still marked with a faint shadow and indentations that will not fade away completely. But I am free now to draw something new and different.

I draw and draw, scattering pages around me like petals dropping off a dying flower. I draw stories. Stories that are only important to me. I draw with abandon. The images scream off my fingers and dance across the page like a slow and sad song. Slightly skewed and imperfect characters living in an unfair world. They look nothing like Lexi Singh's highly styled world of beautiful people. When I copied her style, it wasn't just about leaving myself out of my art. It was also about how I couldn't let myself fully live within it. Now I struggle to capture the pain of every rejection I've ever experienced.

For the first time, I actually want to share my truth. Not just draw it, but share it. With other people. The risk makes my hands shake and my heart pound. If I share *The Froot Loops* with the world, my insides will be turned out. Nothing will be hidden from view.

What if they don't like it? What if they don't like me?

But then again, they don't like me now, so maybe it doesn't matter. I have nothing to lose.

ᐳ　ᐳ　ᐳ

The papers full of my pictures scatter across the bed. The last one, still on my pad, stares back up at me. The main character is no longer blank. She's there, without a mask, fighting injustice and cruelty. It's a picture of a girl with beautiful black hair and dark, intelligent eyes. Her face and body are round, her legs thick and short. She has a look in her eyes that says she has a past and a future. I've finally drawn me. The *real* me.

But nobody understands how much *real* hurts. I curl up on my side in the middle of the papers, closing my eyes. *Real* is waiting in my *Froot Loop* drawings, in all their heart-ripping truth. *Real* tears me open and shows the ugly side of being a high school misfit.

I have to be honest with myself. I can't blame everything that's happened on bullies, or my being fat. So much of it is my fault. I ruled people and things out of my life before I even gave them a chance. I thought I was the one rejected, but maybe it was the opposite. I rejected everyone and everything before they had a chance to show me their true selves. Creating Sienna wasn't about tricking Jesse. Not really. It was about me wanting to look like someone else. There was no grander motive behind it. I wanted to step outside the walls of my skin for a day . . . an hour. And somehow, by becoming someone else, I learned that other people have walls, too. They may not be on the outside like mine, but they are just as hard to break down. Grace isn't a flake. Jesse's not the bully I thought he was, and Dezirea's not a vain diva. We're all so much more than others' narrow perceptions.

I look down at the drawing I just finished. On the page is a school scene, but one where *Froot Loops* reign. The lines are raw and the colors bold. Owen and Grace are on either side of me as I walk down the middle of the hallway. Owen wears an old, wrinkled *Star Trek* T-shirt and his hair is a tousled mass of orange curls that looks like it hasn't been combed in days. Grace wears purple flip-flops and her pink floral backpack. Her T-shirt says *"Froot Loops"* on the front in big black block letters, and I can imagine her smile in real life, when she sees what I've done.

I wear white—a color I always avoid because of my size—and a bright blue cape flies out behind me as I stride down the hallway unashamed and unflinching. There is no mask covering my face. I don't hug the walls, trying to make myself smaller. I'm not hiding from anything.

In the background are the others, crowded into spaces and shadows up and down the locker-filled hall. Cheerleaders. Football players. Beauty queens. Nerds. Outcasts. Student body presidents. Fat. Skinny. Ugly. Beautiful.

The drawing is good. Better than good.

I start to smile. This is what I am supposed to do. I realize I can create a home for myself where my body will relax and feel comfortable. Maybe others like me will feel at home there, too.

I can create a world that others will want to join and explore. It won't be like Mountainview and I won't be like Nosy Parker. Or anyone else. I'll just be me.

        ⌖   ⌖   ⌖

I spend the rest of the weekend drawing pages and pages of stuff. Some of it is good and some of it stinks, but I keep going. My phone is off and I stay away from the internet, coming out of my room only for meals. I tell my mom I have a huge project to finish for school and she buys it because she's busy grading exams.

On Sunday afternoon, I walk into the kitchen, where Mom is fixing herself a tuna sandwich. She's still in her pajamas with her glasses on and her hair up in a bun with a pencil stuck through the middle.

"Would you like a sandwich?" she asks me.

I shake my head. I have no appetite.

"Are you feeling okay, hon?" Mom asks, frowning at me, and I nod quickly.

"Hey, have you talked to Claire's mom lately?" I ask nervously. I hope that to Mom, I sound calm. I fold my arms across my chest, bracing myself for the bad news.

"No, I think she's at a conference in Seattle." Mom pauses to cut her sandwich in half on the diagonal. I breathe a sigh of relief.

Katy Purry winds in and out between her legs, meowing loudly at the smell of the tuna. "That cat is going to kill me one day," Mom adds.

"You and me both," I say, and Mom laughs. I smile. It feels good to hear someone laugh.

"Did I tell you we turned in our grant proposal last week?" She opens the dishwasher and sticks a spoon inside.

"No," I say.

"I actually think we have a great chance of getting it." Mom successfully dodges Katy Purry one more time, then brings the tuna sandwich to the table.

"That's good," I say, sitting down beside her. "Maybe I will have a little of the sandwich."

"Of course," Mom says, handing me a half of the sandwich. "Oh, I almost forgot." She snaps her fingers. "Claire's mom did actually text me something very interesting just last night."

I freeze with the sandwich halfway to my mouth. My stomach flips.

Here it comes.

"She decided not to take the job here in Fort Collins," Mom tells me. "I guess Claire won't be coming to your school after all."

I briefly close my eyes in relief. This good news will only buy me a little time. Sooner or later Claire is going to tell her mother what I did, and then her mother will tell mine. I need to talk to Claire. Even if she doesn't want to talk back.

"Are you sure you're feeling okay?" Mom asks, peering at me over the top of her reading glasses.

"My stomach's a little queasy." It's the truth.

She puts the back of her hand on my forehead, then smooths the hair back from my face. "I don't think you have a temperature, but maybe you should just take it easy this afternoon. Do you want some tea or something?"

I shake my head. "No, but I think I'm going to go back upstairs and lie down."

She nods. "I'll check in on you later."

⌖   ⌖   ⌖

Upstairs in my room, I carefully close my door. I start to dial Claire's number three times, ending the call each time without connecting. I stare at the phone and feel my knees start to tremble.

I can't do it.

My hands are clammy. I wipe them on my jeans and try again. I close my eyes and listen to the sound of my aching heart. I tell myself I'll get through this, but it's so hard to breathe. When I open my eyes, I call again. This time I listen to it ring once.

Twice.

Claire answers on the third ring. "Hello?"

I expected it to go to voice mail. I suddenly don't know what to say even though I practiced it in my head over and over again.

"Claire?" I finally stammer out. "This is Maisie."

"I know who it is." Her voice is angry. I don't blame her. "What do you want? More pictures of me?"

"No," I say, my voice shaking a little. "I want to apologize. I did a stupid thing, and I'm really sorry."

"I don't forgive you." Her voice is taut.

"I understand that. But I still want you to know how very sorry I am. You didn't deserve any of this, and I promise I'll never bother you again."

There is silence on the other end of the phone and for a second I think she may have hung up.

I hear her take in a quick, hard breath. Then she asks, "Why me?"

Her voice breaks and it sounds like she might be crying. I can hear the pain in her voice, and I know there is only one person to blame for her misery.

I exhale heavily. The truth is almost more than I can bear to say. After all, haven't I been the one who's struggled with this reality my whole life? But I have to say it.

"Because of how you look." It is so ugly when I say it aloud.

Her only answer is the click of the line as the phone call disconnects.

�☋ ☋ ☋

That night, while Mom is in the study grading, I walk downstairs and sit on the couch beside my dad.

"Can I talk to you?" I ask.

My dad's eyes don't leave the football game, his hand reaching for the tortilla chips in front of him. "Sure," he says.

"I think I need to stay home from school tomorrow."

He must hear something in my voice. He glances sideways toward me, then points the remote at the television and turns it off. He's looking at me hard enough to make me nervous.

"What's up?" he asks.

I tell my dad I'm sick.

He looks at me. No expression on his face. Somehow, my dad always knows when I'm lying even when my mom doesn't. "No you're not. Why don't you want to go to school?"

"I screwed up. Everybody is mad at me. I did something really stupid."

"Okay. How long you think you'll need to hide out?" he asks.

"I'm not exactly hiding . . ." But I am.

"And when you go back to school, then what?"

I don't want him to be right, but I know he is. I'm still going to have to face what I've done. Tomorrow. Next week. Some time. It's going to happen, so it's better to hit it straight on. Get it over with.

"What did you do?" Dad asks.

"I pretended to be someone online I wasn't. A lot of people were hurt because of what I did."

He raises his eyebrows. "Wow."

"That's it? That's all you're going to say?"

"I'm trying to take it all in."

I nod. "Yeah, it's a lot."

He doesn't ask why or how. And that's exactly why I'm talking to him.

"So how do I fix it?" I ask.

"You can't fix it," Dad says, putting an arm around me and pulling me toward his side. I put my head on his shoulder with a sigh. "You just have to live through it."

☞   ☞   ☞

I can't sleep, of course. I can't stop thinking about what Dad said. Or Claire's reaction to my apology. Just saying I was sorry didn't make everything magically go away.

There are so many other people I need to face, and they are probably going to be just as angry as Claire. Dad is right. I have to live through it.

I sit up in bed. The first step is to go back to the way it all started. Online. I set up my computer on my desk and sit down in front of it, plain-faced and somber. The camera waits, unblinking, for me to hit record, and suddenly it's my face and my voice on the screen. No filters and no strange angles to hide behind. I start to talk, slowly at first, my words stilted and formal.

"I'm sorry for hurting people by pretending to be someone else. It was wrong. I shouldn't have lied, and for that I truly apologize. From now on, I only want to be honest. I want to be myself. This is the best way I can show you my true self, and that comes with lots of thorns and ugliness. None of us can create perfection. We are flawed in different ways, but we are all flawed."

I take a deep, shaky breath, thinking for a moment about Dezirea and Jesse, and then continue. "I also learned something else. Sometimes the things we hide are wonderful talents and kind hearts that go unnoticed by the rest of the world."

My eyes fill up with tears, but I blink them away.

"I want to share something with you all. Something very real to me and incredibly personal—my drawings. I hope all the Froot Loops in the world will understand. You know who you are."

I turn off the camera and just sit for a moment, breathing in and breathing out. Everything inside me feels shaky and fragile, but before I can chicken out, I upload the video to ChitChat. Then I post all my strips—ones with regular people, and ones with dragons and Labrador retrievers and wolves and monsters. None of them are sophisticated and stylish. They are raw and visceral. The frames around each strip are uneven and torn.

When it is done, I reach for the lamp on my nightstand, but then I change my mind and leave it on. I don't want to be in the dark anymore.

CHAPTER TWENTY-SIX

On Monday morning, I throw on some jeans and a white T-shirt, adding a long black cardigan over the top. Nothing colorful today. No mixed prints or bright, cheerful shades. I pull my hair back into a low pony and grab a clip off the top of my dresser. It's time to face the music. It's the least I can do.

Owen has a dentist appointment early this morning, so I don't need to pick him up. I drive to school alone, then park in the student lot, waiting. I watch from my car as kids stream toward the school. The sun is peeking above the foothills, casting long golden rays of light across the sky. I sit in the driver's seat, windows cracked. My fingers tap restlessly on the steering wheel. *Ten more minutes*, I tell myself.

When I finally step out of the car, Grace is suddenly there beside me. I look at her and force a smile. All I can think of is how grateful I am to see her. She knows how horrible I've been, but she still looks me in the eye. When she smiles at me, my eyes fill up with tears. I never knew how much kindness can mean when I least expect it. When I least deserve it. Somehow, some way, I vow to pass on this compassion.

"I thought you might need some company," she says.

How could I have ever doubted that Grace is perfect for Owen?

"Thank you," I whisper. Grace grabs my hand. I don't pull away. Together we walk into the school. Heads turn to look at me. Eyes glare.

I walk with Grace down the hall to my locker, drowning in the hatred and whispered comments surrounding us. I wrap my black cardigan tighter around my body. Every step is difficult. It feels like I'm breathing water into my lungs instead of air. All I have to do is survive this moment to get through to the next. I fight for every breath, feeling the poisoned looks close over my head and the current sucking me under.

I look over at Grace and her eyes say, *Swim*.

I know she is trying to help, but I have to face the consequences of my deception alone. I deserve the looks and more. The fact that everyone is judging me for what I did feels awful, but that isn't what makes my heart break apart. That will come soon, when I walk into class and see Jesse again.

In chemistry, my heels tap against the tiled floor as I trudge toward the front of the room. I squeeze my way through the tables toward the empty stool. The snickers and whispers start up as everyone monitors my progress. They spread across the room and grow louder the closer I get to my seat. Everyone watches, conversations stopping.

Jesse's stool is empty. I look over my shoulder and see him now sitting beside Casey Austin. Evidently he had a private conversation with Mr. Vance persuasive enough to move him to a new lab partner. I don't want to think about what he said, but I can't help but wonder.

"Can I sit here?" Owen slides onto the empty stool beside me. He places his familiar, beat-up green backpack on the floor between us, next to his meticulously white sneakers. I've never been so happy to see someone in my life. I nod, not able to trust my voice to respond.

He pushes something across the desk toward me. I look down to see a small white candle in a blue jar. I raise my eyebrows in question.

"Candles are an essential element in hygge. In Danish they are called *levende lys*, which means *living light*. You really can't have a *hyggelig* night without them."

"Thank you," I say. I smile then—the first real one all day. "I'll be sure and burn it tonight."

"Smell," he says, and I lift it up to my nose, inhaling the magical scent deeply.

"Aromatherapy. It's lavender and frankincense to calm the chatter in your head."

"I hope it works," I say, thinking the chatter in my head sounds more like screaming right now, but maybe hygge will work its magic.

Somehow, I manage to make it through class. I sit stone-faced and silent. That is okay with me. I don't want to talk to anyone. Especially not Jesse Santos.

When the bell rings, Jesse is off the stool and into the aisle before I can even put away my notebook. Dezirea and Camila are there instantly, smiling and taking his arm to escort him out of the room and back into society, where he belongs. I watch him walk down the hall, his long legs keeping in time with Dezirea's high-heeled boots. He looks at her and she laughs up into his face. My stomach crawls.

Outside, I part ways with Owen, and then I lean against the lockers, my hand on my pounding chest. It hurts. Not like when you fall down and skin your knee. It's more like a huge, sucking emptiness that makes you wish you could bleed so people would recognize the hurt. If I was bleeding, nurses would run out of the ER yelling out for a transfusion stat. But this kind of hurt is different.

I have to get out of here before I lose it in front of the whole school. I pick up my backpack and head for the girls' bathroom, blinking rapidly.

They will not see me cry. They will not see me cry.

I turn on the water in the sink and let it run. The mirror is cracked from side to side, fracturing my face into tiny, ripped shreds. My eyes are wide and devastated, and I can't see myself beyond them. I have no one but myself to blame. No one made me change into someone else but me.

The bathroom door opens and I think it will be Grace, but instead I see Dezirea in the mirror. She flops a bag on the countertop and pulls out a lipstick. I lower my eyes and pump some soap onto my hands.

Out of the corner of my eye I see her applying a thick coat of gloss on her lips, then fluffing her hair. She glances my way, and I look around frantically for the paper towels.

"You okay?" she asks.

At first I'm not sure she's talking to me, but there's no one else here. I savagely yank out a paper towel.

My eyes fill up with tears, making me even angrier. I wipe frantically at my eyes. "I'm fine," I say, throwing the towel in the trash and turning to leave.

"Wait," she says.

I turn around slowly. She looks at me. Really looks.

She leans back against the green tiled wall. Cross-legged, her bag in between her legs, she says, "Lock the door."

I stop, hand on the door. Instead of opening it, I lock it. I turn around slowly.

She puts her hands on her hips and stares at me from under her long eyelashes. "I *should* be mad at you."

Dezirea is speaking. To. Me. My heart thumps in my chest.

"I know," I say. "But you're not?"

"Your drawings are cool." I honestly can't believe what I'm hearing.

Her voice is quiet as she continues. "Sometimes I think I'm only powerful because of the way I look. Your drawings made me *feel* powerful. Like I could do anything."

"Is that a compliment?" I ask.

She lifts one shoulder in a shrug. "Yeah."

Tears well up in my eyes, but I blink them back. I think of a lot of responses, but I just say, "Thank you."

"I'm not stupid."

Suddenly I find it hard to breathe. I stare at her, mouth open. "I never thought you were."

"So why did we quit talking to each other?" she asks.

"I don't know, but it wasn't because I thought you were stupid," I say. "Never that."

"Sometimes you look at me, and I think you hate me."

I frown. "I never knew you saw me. I thought I was invisible to you."

She laughs. "I guess we're not the best mind readers, are we?"

I shake my head.

Dezirea is quiet for a moment. "At first I couldn't believe Sienna was *you*," she says. "But then I started thinking about it. And I realized that Sienna reminded me of the you I used to know. The you at sleepovers and birthday parties. The you in the mountains under a sky full of stars."

"You remember that?" I ask incredulously.

"Of course I do." She laughs. "You were always a good listener."

"Sienna *was* me . . . sort of." I swallow hard and lick my lips. "She made it easier for me to talk to other people. And listen."

"Yeah," Dezirea says softly.

"I'm sorry about your parents' divorce. I didn't know."

She stretches her hands up above her head. "I don't talk about it much," she finally says.

I nod. I understand that part. There's a lot I don't talk about. "We were true friends once, weren't we?"

Dezirea nods, then lets her head rest against the wall. "You shouldn't stop."

"Stop what?"

"Drawing your stories. They . . . say something important," she says.

"You keep dancing," I tell her, giving her a small smile.

"You keep drawing," she says.

I put my fist out into the space between us with my pinkie finger up. She does the same. Our little fingers entwine and we shake on it.

Dezirea leaves the bathroom first. After she's gone, I think about our conversation. I never really hated Dezirea. In fact, I like her. She isn't perfect.

I like Jesse. He isn't perfect.

Nobody is perfect. Least of all me.

CHITCHAT DIRECT MESSAGE

LEXI: HI, MAISIE.

OMG. Lexi Singh just sent me a message. Me!!! Personally!!

ME: HI.

LEXI: LOVE THE NEW STUFF YOU POSTED! I WANT MORE!

I can't believe it. *Did she really just say that?*

ME: OH WOW. THANK YOU!

LEXI: DID YOU THINK ABOUT WHAT I SAID?

How could I not?

ME: YES!

LEXI: THEN GET TO WORK! GET BETTER, IMPROVE,
GROW, AND DON'T BE STOPPED BY WHAT OTHERS
THINK OF YOU.

ME: I'M TRYING.

LEXI: MAKE THOSE CHARACTERS LEAP OFF THE PAGE.

CHAPTER TWENTY-SEVEN

It is two weeks after Sienna left for good. Inspired by Lexi's praise, I've joined an online comics board, and I post the *Froot Loops* strip regularly. The response from other artists is surprising. I never knew there were so many people out there who felt the same way I do. And that's been amazing.

The truth is, I can't forget the way I felt when I created my escape: Sienna. I can't forget the words that belonged to me, yet to someone else entirely. But Sienna left me with some of her confidence, and I've started to believe I can be me for real. From the inside out. Maybe it's good to have a broken heart. Some broken things need to be broken further before they can heal. At least I feel something. And something is better than nothing. It means I cared.

I still do.

Things could be better, but they could be so much worse. I survive by concentrating on putting one foot in front of the other during the day, and drawing my heart out onto the page every night by the scent of my hygge candle. I remind myself, surrounded by the calming smell of lavender and frankincense, that no matter how far away I slipped with Sienna, I was still Maisie inside.

And now I'm becoming Maisie on the outside, too. I don't flinch away. I don't cower in hallways, afraid to bump into people. I wear purple and pink and even yellow. Sometimes all at once. When people look at me, I stare right back. I am trying to stop beating myself up and telling myself hateful things about my body. That's a start.

But there is one thing I still need to do.

On Friday morning, I wait for Jesse outside of chemistry class. He looks at me, waiting for me to move out of the way, but I don't.

"Can I talk to you?" I ask.

"You're talking," he says. He is not going to make this easy on me.

"Fine," I say. "Look, I want to apologize for . . ." I don't even know where to start. "Everything."

Jesse's jaw tightens, and after a moment of silence, he speaks. "You lied to me," he says, not meeting my eyes. "I saw you in class every day. You never once told me the truth."

"It was all true except for the pictures."

Jesse looks skeptical. "Right," he says sarcastically. "Like how much you just love jazz."

"I do now," I say.

"But you're not Sienna," he says quietly. "And she's not you."

"I don't want to be her. I want to be me," I say quietly. "Inside and outside."

"Good luck with that." He says it like that settles things, then turns to walk away.

"Wait." I put my hand on his arm to stop him from leaving, and I can feel the warmth of his skin. I flinch away as though it burns. "Please?"

He turns around and looks at me for a long time, his dark eyes sad.

"Why did you do it?" he finally asks.

There it is. The million-dollar question. The one that's been banging around in my head like a hammer.

Why?

There is a tiny pause while I try out answers in my head. None of them will work.

"I didn't mean for it to go that far," I say at last.

He stares back at me blankly. We both know that's not an answer. I take a deep breath and try again.

"I didn't like you very much." The words burn in my mouth.

"So you pretended to be someone else just to hurt me."

What I did to him suddenly hits me like a kick to my stomach. I press the palms of my hands to my forehead. Then I nod.

"So I deserved it? Is that what you're saying?" His voice is angry, his eyes narrow. "What did I do to deserve it?"

That I can try to answer. "Think about it," I say. "The years of teasing? The Froot-Loops-in-the-locker incident? That was bad."

I wait until he thinks about it. He stares at the floor. Finally, something changes in his face, and after a moment he nods again. "You're right," he says. "It was. And I'm really sorry." Then he looks up, meets my eyes, and says, "Sometimes it's easier to just go with the crowd." He gives me a sad, sideways grin. "And to be honest? I did a lot of those silly things to get your attention. I was immature and stupid and I *liked* you."

I'm confused. My head is spinning. "You liked me?" I ask, my stomach doing flip-flops.

"Yeah," Jesse says with a sheepish smile.

"Why?" Now it's my turn to ask that question.

"Because you were . . . are . . . creative and smart and funny."

Now I'm the one who is shocked. My heart is beating so loud, I can hardly speak. "You can't tell me you actually liked me *before* Sienna?"

"I did. Maybe not in the same way, but I liked you. I admired you. I thought you were cool."

Jesse Santos thought I was *cool*? My mouth goes dry.

"You know," I say. "Showing a girl you like her by being a jerk is never a good idea."

Jesse dips his head again. "Yeah. I know that now. I've grown up a lot. I mean, I hope I have. I'm trying."

I take a deep breath. "That's a start. And I *am* really sorry for everything I did," I tell him again. "Do you think you'll ever forgive me?"

He doesn't answer right away. "I don't know," he says at last. "I need time."

"I get that," I say.

The bell rings, and we walk into class. I head for my desk, but then Jesse says, "I read your comics."

I glance at him. "Which one?"

"All of them."

"Oh," I say, because I don't know what else to say.

"They helped me understand some things."

I hold my breath, just letting him speak.

"Not everything," he adds. "But some things."

I let out a breath. "I'm glad," I say.

"Yeah," Jesse says, and he gives me another small smile.

That *is* a start.

☞   ☞   ☞

Instead of going to the cafeteria for lunch, I sit on the Thinking Bench. I pull out my old drawing of the fairy. The one I asked to make me not care. Now I know better.

Caring is messy and painful and stupid and . . . worth it. Worth everything.

I want to draw something new. I turn to a new page. The images slip off my fingers and dance across the page like a slow and sad song. The lines I sketch are rounded. The vision is clear. I know who will be in this picture.

Me.

MAISIE FERNANDEZ'S COMICS PAGE

COMMENT BELOW!

EVEN THOUGH I'M A STRANGER TO YOU . . . YOUR DRAWINGS MAKE ME FEEL LIKE YOU'RE NOT A STRANGER TO ME. #FROOTLOOPS4EVER

I'VE NEVER TOLD ANYONE ABOUT HOW I FEEL ABOUT MYSELF, BUT YOU MAKE ME FEEL LIKE SOMEONE UNDERSTANDS. THANK YOU. #FROOTLOOPS4EVER

FROOT LOOPS EVERYWHERE UNITE TO FIGHT THE MOST IMPORTANT BATTLE OF ALL: THE ONE AGAINST OUR OWN INTERNAL INSECURITIES. #FROOTLOOPS4EVER

I ALWAYS TRY TO BE INVISIBLE, BUT IT'S HARD WHEN YOU'RE THE FATTEST PERSON IN THE ROOM. NOT ANYMORE! #FROOTLOOPS4EVER

FINALLY, SOMEONE GETS ME. #FROOTLOOPS4EVER

YOU MAKE ME FEEL LESS ISOLATED AND ALONE. THANKS FOR THAT! #FROOTLOOPS4EVER

ACKNOWLEDGMENTS

Thank you first to my readers. You made my dreams of being an author come true in such an amazing way and I am so grateful every day.

Thank you to Aimee Friedman, for her continued support and guidance. I couldn't have asked for a better editor. My appreciation to all the wonderful people at Scholastic who worked so hard to bring this book to life—David Levithan, Tracy van Straaten, Rachel Feld, Shannon Pender, Lizette Serrano, Emily Heddleson, Yaffa Jaskoll, Caroline Flanagan, Caitlin Mahon, Jackie Hornberger, Carson Lombardi, Kerianne Steinberg, Maria Chang, Olivia Valcarce, Mariclaire Jastremsky, and everyone in the Book Fairs, Book Clubs, and Sales.

I cannot express the extent of my gratitude to my agent, Sarah Davies at Greenhouse Literary Agency. She had faith in my storytelling abilities when I did not and she continues to guide me with wisdom and kindness.

Fortunately, I have an amazing support system of writers and friends who constantly encourage me. My eternal gratitude to Kathi Appelt, Debbie Leland, Talia Vance, Bret Ballou, Katy Longshore, Veronica Rossi, Beth Hull, Kristen Held, Karmen Kelly, Rod Lucero, Derek Decker, Joy Decker, Greg Rattenborg, and Karen Rattenborg.

Thanks also to my entire family for fostering my love of books and writing. My husband, Jay, keeps my real world working when I'm deep in an imaginary one and it is deeply appreciated.

Finally, I miss you, Mom. Every. Day.

Books about Love.
Books about Life.
Books about You.

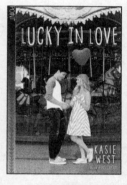

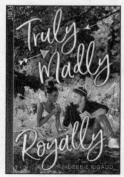

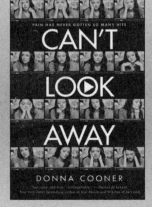